"What about you? You interested in having children someday?"

Ivy's eyes filled with pain. "I don't think I'm meant for that," she mumbled.

"Well, that makes two of us," he said, needing instinctively to erase that pain.

"Really? You don't want a family of your own?"

"The way I look at it," Ryan explained carefully, "I already have one. My students mean a lot to me." He smiled. "You might even say my devotion to my work has gotten a bit out of hand. I spend most of my time occupied with coaching, administrating and just spending time with the students. Some of them desperately need an adult who will listen."

Ivy tilted her head. "Is that enough for you? Listening to someone else's kids? I used to think work was enough, too."

"Not anymore?"

She pondered that before shaking her head. "No," she said softly. "Not anymore. Family is everything."

Books by Arlene James

Love Inspired

**The Perfect Wedding*
**An Old-Fashioned Love*
**A Wife Worth Waiting For*
**With Baby in Mind*
To Heal a Heart
Deck the Halls
A Family to Share
Butterfly Summer
A Love So Strong
When Love Comes Home
A Mommy in Mind
***His Small-Town Girl*
***Her Small-Town Hero*
***Their Small-Town Love*

*Everyday Miracles
**Eden, OK

ARLENE JAMES

says, "Camp meetings, mission work and church attendance permeate my Oklahoma childhood memories. It was a golden time, which sustains me yet. However, only as a young, widowed mother did I truly begin growing in my personal relationship with the Lord. Through adversity, He has blessed me in countless ways, one of which is a second marriage so loving and romantic it still feels like courtship!"

The author of more than sixty novels, Arlene James now resides outside of Fort Worth, Texas, with her beloved husband. Her need to write is greater than ever, a fact that frankly amazes her, as she's been at it since the eighth grade! She loves to hear from readers, and can be reached at 1301 E. Debbie Lane, Suite 102, Box 117, Mansfield, Texas 76063, or via her Web site at www.arlenejames.com.

Their Small-Town Love

Arlene James

Published by Steeple Hill Books™

STEEPLE HILL BOOKS

ISBN-13: 978-0-373-81394-0
ISBN-10: 0-373-81394-5

THEIR SMALL-TOWN LOVE

This edition published by arrangement with Steeple Hill Books.

www.SteepleHill.com

Printed in U.S.A.

And after you have suffered for a little,
the God of all grace, who called you to
His eternal glory in Christ, will Himself perfect,
confirm, strengthen and establish you. To Him
be dominion forever and ever. Amen.

—1 *Peter* 5:10–11

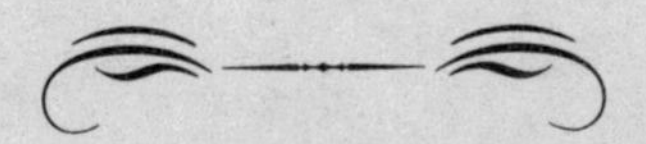

Chapter One

It looked just the same.

Ivy let the hunter green, barn-style door slowly swing closed behind her as she surveyed the homey lobby of the Heavenly Arms Motel. Hap's old rocking chair still sat before the potbellied stove in the corner, and the game table, its surface worn by the shuffle of countless dominoes, still claimed center stage. On closer inspection, one of the black leather couches appeared to be a replacement for a former version, but it all *felt* just as she recalled, much more of a living room than a motel lobby, despite the chest-high counter behind her.

In nearly seven years, nothing appeared to have changed, not at the motel and apparently not in her hometown of Eden, Oklahoma. On the one hand, Ivy found that comforting; on the other hand, she prayed that this was not a harbinger of things to come.

The sound of a door opening made Ivy turn just as a petite blonde in slender jeans and a striped T-shirt emerged from the office to smile across the counter at her. Ivy masked her surprise, partly relieved and partly disappointed. She'd expected Charlotte or one of the other Jeffords. The presence of this small, pretty stranger demonstrated that some things had changed around here, after all.

"Hello. Can I help you?" the blonde asked, swinging a chunky toddler onto her trim hip. Dressed in olive-green corduroy overalls and a bright yellow T-shirt, the boy twinkled blue eyes at Ivy, expecting instant acceptance.

Ivy smiled, despite the pang in her chest, and addressed the blonde. "I have a reservation."

The woman seemed relieved. "That's good. We've booked a full house." As she pulled a registration form from beneath the counter, she asked, "Here for the reunion?"

Ivy accepted an ink pen and began to fill in the required information as best she could. "That's right. The reunion." *More than one, hopefully.*

"Seems to be a big deal around here," the blonde went on.

That, Ivy thought, *is an understatement.*

The annual high school reunion, always scheduled for the Saturday before Easter, counted as one of the highlights of the year in the small town of Eden and had for as long as Ivy could remember. Tonight's banquet would be the first that thirty-year-old Ivy had attended, however. In the twelve years since she had graduated from Eden Memorial High School, she had returned to her hometown only rarely—and not at all for more than six years.

Truth be told, she'd gladly have skipped tonight's festivities, had they not been her excuse for returning after all this time. She trembled a little, recalling her father's last words to her.

"If you have any shred of decency left, you won't ever show your face around here again. You've got nothing to say that I want to hear, so don't bother calling or writing, either."

She had honored his wishes and had planned to keep doing so—until several months ago when she'd found herself on her knees in a break room at the radio station where she'd worked in Tulsa. The good friend who had knelt with her had held her hand as Ivy wept and confessed to God her many failings.

In the time since, Ivy's world had literally turned on its head. She learned that God's forgiveness removed the eternal ramifications of her sin and that she owed it to herself and others to try to make amends to anyone she'd ever harmed. But how did she approach someone who never wanted to see her again, let alone ask for his forgiveness? She already knew that turning her life over to God did not mean that everything would suddenly become perfect. Quite the opposite in some respects. It could make, and had made, life very difficult. Then again, most of the mess was of her own making.

Ivy pushed the form back across the counter and smiled at the pretty hotel clerk. “I’m sorry, but I don’t have a permanent address at the moment.”

The woman glanced down at what was written on the form before saying, “Oh, that’s all right, Ms. Villard. Your credit card has been approved, and that’s what counts. Welcome back, by the way.”

That might well be the only welcome she would receive, Ivy mused. She hoped, prayed, that her sister, Rose, would be glad to see her, but their father undoubtedly would not be. Ivy expected that he would refuse to meet with her. Still, she had to try. He had been right, after all, about everything.

Ivy had elected not to inform Rose of her plans to attend the reunion, despite their recent tentative communication via e-mail. As much as Ivy would have liked to prepare her younger sister for seeing her unexpectedly after all these years, she knew that she would do better to protect Rose from their father’s anger. Should Olie conclude that Rose had participated in, or even kept mum about Ivy’s plan to see him, he might well cut Rose and her family from his life as he had Ivy. It seemed best to just show up where she expected her sister to be and let matters proceed from there. Or not, as God willed.

Forcing her thoughts back to the young woman across the counter from her, Ivy pulled out her best manners. “Thank you. That’s very kind. Do you mind if I ask your name?”

"Oh." The blonde ducked her head shyly, hunching her slender shoulders. "Sorry. I'm Cara." She laid a key on the counter and offered her tiny hand, saying, "Number four ought to suit you."

Ivy accepted the other woman's hand, clasping it briefly with her own. "Nice to meet you, Cara. Do you mind if I also ask about the Jeffords?"

"Not at all."

"Do they still own the place, then?"

Cara laughed. "Absolutely. Although Hap is thinking about retiring when Charlotte and her husband get their house finished."

"Charlotte's married?" Ivy asked, pleasantly surprised. Charlotte had always seemed utterly dedicated to the care of her grandfather.

"She married Tyler Aldrich," Cara said, rocking back on her heels as if to give the words greater significance.

Ivy could only shake her head. "I'm afraid I don't know a Tyler Aldrich. I've been gone a long time, you see. Is he new to the area?"

Cara chuckled. "Oh, yes. The Aldrich family hail from Dallas. Maybe you've heard of the Aldrich grocery store chain?"

"*That* Tyler Aldrich?" Ivy straightened, blinking. It all but boggled the mind, to think of mild, dutiful Charlotte married to the Aldrich fortune.

Cara nodded, grinning. "He is such a nice a man."

Before Ivy could inquire further, the telephone

rang, and Cara hurried to answer it, tossing an apologetic smile over her shoulder. Ivy slid the key into the outer pocket of her soft, roomy leather handbag and left the other woman to her business. The child on Cara's hip watched Ivy as she turned away. He watched still when Ivy glanced back, one hand on the door, as if he sensed the longing in her, bone-deep, forever unfulfilled. Bag clutched under her arm, she gave him a wistful little wave and went out into the blustery, late-March afternoon.

Wind spun her long dark hair about her face as she hurried toward the small, boxy SUV hybrid that she'd left parked under the drive-through. Its bronze-brown body and darkly tinted windows hid the fact that it carried the majority of her earthly possessions, everything she hadn't sold, given away or put into storage before embarking upon a new life.

She tossed the big, puffy handbag into the passenger seat atop the small suitcase she had packed for what would undoubtedly be a short stay here in Eden. Holding closed the sides of the long, tailored tan jacket that she wore over comfortable black leggings and a pretty, babydoll top, she slid beneath the steering wheel and set the flat sole of one calf-high boot against the brake peddle. A sultry warmth already softened the edge of the stirring breeze, so the boots would soon have to be retired for the season.

Easter had come early this year, but as always it

brought spring with it, an appropriate time for, God willing, renewal. It seemed right to journey out on faith, trusting that if the job for which she had applied at the radio station in Oklahoma City did not come through, something else would. Thankfully, Ivy still had connections in this part of the state, though explaining the break-up of the *Fire-Brand Phillips and Ivy* radio show was proving difficult. Still, being half of what had once been one of the most popular programs on commercial "rock/talk" radio didn't hurt.

Except that it had. Did.

It was never easy when you turned out to be exactly the fool that others had claimed.

She had reason to hope, though. As sorry as she was for the wrong choices she had made in the past and as willing to atone for them, she knew in Whom she had placed her faith, and she trusted Him to bring a brighter future. Perhaps it would never be what she had once dreamed it might, but she was content to do her best and leave the rest to her Lord.

Yes, she very much wanted to see her sister, to hear the sound of her voice and be enfolded in her embrace. Most of all, she wanted to recognize welcome in Rose's tawny brown eyes—but what would be, would be. With God's help, Ivy could survive her disappointment if Rose turned her back. She had survived before when their father had done the same, but this time she would not be all on her own. Never again would she be all on her own, even if she should forever be alone as "Fire-Brand" had predicted.

As she donned her little black dress with its flirty, knee-length hem and crisscrossing spaghetti straps that so closely matched those of her spiked heels, Ivy imagined the look of surprise that she would undoubtedly see on Rose's face. She prayed that she would also see pleasure and welcome there—and that ultimately her father would agree to meet with her, as well. She asked for the right words to say and the right tone to take and for strength and grace in what would surely be a difficult moment.

Ivy never expected that when she finally laid eyes on her sister again, she would find Rose obviously pregnant with her third child or that the depth of pain and envy that she would feel at the sight of that big rounded belly would diminish the much-anticipated joy of her only sister's loving embrace.

As assistant principal, history teacher and all-around coach, Ryan Jefford was well-known around the alma mater, a permanent fixture, some said. He liked it that way. After college he had returned to Eden and devoted himself to educating the youth of his hometown. It was a decision he hadn't regretted so far.

He loved these yearly Easter-weekend reunions,

delighted in seeing his old classmates and, at the advanced age of thirty-four, even former students. Easily recognizable even in the soft light from the candles that glittered around the decorated cafeteria, he'd long been the unofficial host of these annual events, no matter the ever-changing composition of the committee in charge. As he worked his way through the milling, chattering throng, dispensing handshakes, backslaps and smiles, he felt a sense of pride in this place and all who had passed through it over the years, and that definitely included his older brother, whom Ryan spied in the distance.

At six foot four and a half, Holt tended to stand out in a crowd. It came as no surprise to see Holt's pretty, petite wife, Cara, beaming at her husband's side. Ryan wondered if she'd stopped smiling even once in the three weeks since their wedding. As he moved toward them, he saw that his sister, Charlotte, and brother-in-law, Ty, also stood nearby, surrounded by a crowd of curious alumni anxious to meet the wealthy grocery store magnate.

Ty seemed politely amused by the interest, while a surprisingly polished Charlotte looked on with subdued pride. Ryan chuckled to himself, imagining that some of those gathered around Tyler were disappointed to find that such a wealthy man seemed so ordinary and down-to-earth. That everyman persona could be a tad misleading, however, as Tyler Aldrich could, and did, get things done with great speed and ease. Only a few weeks ago, he'd helped Cara and Holt settle a tricky custody battle with her late husband's parents with a single phone call and, in Ty's stated opinion, a modest check. It hadn't hurt that Holt and Cara had quickly married, either, ostensibly to provide her delightful baby boy, Ace, with a stable, two-parent home. In truth, Holt and Cara were as deeply in love as Charlotte and Ty, and Ryan took no small measure of credit for having helped them realize it.

Now everyone said that Ryan's turn had come to take that much-vaunted hike down the aisle, but Ryan doubted that. He remembered the difficulties of his parents' marriage and knew too well the great time demands of his calling. As an educator, he took his work very seriously. He loved his family, and they truly came first in his heart, but he had to admit that their needs often came second to those of his students and school. His family and his passion for education centered his life, just as his faith, church and convictions centered his spirit. He simply had nothing left over for romance. After what love had cost his mother—her life—he was okay without it. Fortunately, he found great contentment in his work.

"Looking sharp there, Mr. Jefford," his big brother greeted him, flicking the lapel of Ryan's black suit.

Ryan straightened the knot of his silk tie, grass green in keeping with the school colors. He had a yellow one, as well as several yellow-and-green striped varieties, at home in his closet, but the reunion committee always went with yellow rosebud boutonnieres, so he routinely chose the green silk for these events.

"You're looking better than usual yourself," he said to Holt, then bent slightly to wink at his sister-in-law. "Well done, Cara."

She laughed while Holt rolled his eyes, but he snaked an arm around his bride's slender shoulders in clear possession of the pretty blonde. Ryan smiled to see it. Holt and Cara's helpless, starry-eyed delight in each other pleased Ryan as much as Charlotte and Ty's settled contentment. An old married couple of almost four months, Charlotte and her husband had displayed a firm, harmonious ease from the beginning, despite the vast differences in their backgrounds.

Distracted momentarily by the chairwoman of the reunion committee who wanted to make sure that he was prepared to welcome the returning alumni as soon as they sat down to dinner, Ryan turned away from his siblings—and saw Ivy Villard.

He knew her at once, although it had been many years since he'd last laid eyes on her. Back then she'd been wearing a green-and-yellow cheerleader's uniform, not so different from those that the girls serving the tables wore tonight. For some reason, she was the very last person he'd have expected to attend the reunion. Yet there she sat at a table with her sister, Rose, and brother-in-law, Daniel Halsey, a teacher and baseball coach at the junior high school.

She looked almost the same, her long dark hair hanging straight down her back, a perfect frame for her slender oval face and big, deeply set, cinnamon-brown eyes. Her cunningly simple dress emphasized an edge of sophistication and maturity, honed, no doubt, by the years that had passed. The dusky tone of her creamy skin gave testament to her Native American ancestry, which he knew came from her maternal grandmother, and called attention to the shimmering, pale-pink lipstick that adorned her lips.

He'd thought her pretty back in high school. Now she was nothing less than stunning, and he wondered what she'd been doing with herself all these years. He wasn't the only one to notice her.

"Isn't that Ivy?" Charlotte asked, coming to stand beside him.

"I believe it is."

"Who's Ivy?" Tyler asked, appearing at Charlotte's other side.

"Used to be head cheerleader around here," Holt supplied. "She was, what, two or three years ahead of you, sis?"

"Three," Ryan said. "Class of '96."

"Oh, I know her!" Cara exclaimed. "She's staying at the motel."

Ryan raised an eyebrow at this news. Why, he wondered, did she not stay with her father? It occurred to him then that he hadn't seen Olie Villard in some time. He'd seen and heard even less of Ivy. Now Ryan wondered just how the old man fared, and if some difficulty with him might account for Ivy's sudden reappearance after all these years. Concerned, he addressed his brother.

"Have you seen Olie around lately?"

Holt shook his head. "He's always been one to keep to himself. I have heard, though, that he's attending the Magnolia church with Rose and her family."

The church on Magnolia Avenue, which happened to be situated quite near Ryan's house, was a "plant" of First Church, which, being landlocked, could no longer meet the needs of its burgeoning congregation. The pastor at First Church, Grover Waller, had encouraged several young families to consider transferring to Magnolia Christian in order to help support that fledgling congregation and its young pastor, Davis Latimer. Ryan had considered making the move himself, but the Jefford family had been members of First Church for three generations.

Ryan couldn't resist the urge to glance back in Ivy's direction. "You don't suppose Olie's ill, do you?"

Holt's expression grew troubled. "He didn't

look well the last time I saw him, but with Olie it's hard to tell."

Not the most pleasant of men, Olie had always worn a rather sour expression. Some said he'd been that way since his wife had abandoned the family many years earlier. Ryan just barely remembered the woman himself, but he knew that Ivy had resented her. He'd once overheard her say, with that certainty peculiar to teenagers, that it would have been easier for everyone if her mother had died when Ivy was a baby rather than just take off and leave her.

Ryan vehemently opposed that notion himself, since his own mother had taken her life after his father had died in an oil field accident when he was twenty. That experience had been anything but easy, though it had all happened long ago, almost fourteen years. Shocked to realize that it had been at least that long since he had last spoken to Ivy, he decided to rectify the situation.

"I'll be back."

"But you just got here," Holt protested. Ryan ignored him and fixed his gaze on Ivy's table as he made his way through the chattering throng. He could visit with his siblings anytime. This might be his only chance to catch up with Ivy Villard, and suddenly that seemed much more important.

"You haven't changed a bit."

Ivy looked up. This was not the first time she'd

heard that particular sentiment tonight. It was, of course, less than accurate, but at thirty she was old enough to appreciate hearing it. She was not sure how she recognized this particular former schoolmate, however, for he had changed immensely. She recalled a tall, thin young man with large features and extremities and too much thick, wavy, golden brown hair. He'd grown into those features, and those hands and feet no longer looked like they belonged to someone else. Even the hair fit now. Ivy smiled.

"Hello, Ryan Jefford, and thank you."

Ryan's oddly familiar hazel eyes warmed. "It's good to see you, Ivy. It's been too long."

"Yes. Yes, it has," she agreed, shifting sideways to drape an arm across the back of her folding chair. She let her gaze sweep down and then up again. "You don't look anything like your brother or Hap," she told him. "I saw Holt standing over there and knew him at once."

Ryan chuckled. "I take after our other grandfather, Michael Carl Ryan, or so I'm told. Seems appropriate since I'm named after him."

"He must have been a handsome man," she said bluntly, making a show of reading his name from the badge pinned to his chest, "because you, Ryan Carl Jefford, look great."

Inclining his head in thanks, Ryan said, "Well, then, that makes two of us, Ivy Madeline Villard."

She laughed. To her surprise, he pulled out the

chair on her right and sat down. After exchanging words of greeting with Rose, he began to chat with Daniel about an upcoming track-and-field event, allowing Ivy a moment to take stock of the familiar-yet-unfamiliar man beside her.

In high school, she had found Ryan to be a very nice guy, but rather stolid and even a little boring. She no longer trusted the judgment of the foolish young woman she had been, however. That former version of herself had chosen the flash and dash of Brand Phillips—he wasn't called "FireBrand" for nothing—over any chance of marriage and family.

Looking back, she marveled at how easily she had jettisoned the idea of a normal, responsible life. She could not even claim that she hadn't known what she was doing. Brand had made no secret of the fact that he considered marriage and parenthood unnecessary, confining, boring and a trap. He'd only promised her a grand adventure and she had to admit that he had delivered, but at what a high, painful cost to her!

For one horrible moment, Ivy suddenly hovered on the verge of tears. The pain never seemed to leave her for long or diminish in intensity. Ryan turned to her then and stunned her by seeming to read, with appalling ease, the distress that she had hidden for so very long. Abandoning the discussion with her brother-in-law, he reached toward her, his big, solid hand covering hers lightly.

"You okay?" His hazel eyes peering intently into her darker ones. Blinking, Ivy said nothing for several seconds before he went on. "I can't help wondering if all is well or if some problem has brought you back just in time for the reunion?"

"Problem?" she echoed.

"Is your father all right?" he asked, wondering what troubled this beautiful woman whom he remembered only as a teen.

Ivy swung her gaze back to him, her mouth opened to blurt that she wouldn't know, but then Rose jumped in, the stylish cut of her nut-brown hair swinging jauntily above her shoulders as she nodded. "Dad is fine," she supplied.

"Looking forward to another grandchild," Daniel added, smoothing a hand over his wife's distended belly.

Ryan chuckled, and Ivy felt his hand relax atop hers just before he took it away. "Home to greet the new baby, then?"

"Not exactly," Ivy hedged.

"That is," Rose interjected uncertainly, "the baby is still two months or better away."

Ivy frowned, her gaze going at once to Rose's greatly expanded waistline. Although shorter and sturdier than her, Rose looked much too large to be eight or more weeks away from giving birth.

"Are you sure you're not having twins?" Ryan joked, apparently agreeing with Ivy's assessment.

Rose crinkled her pert nose. "It's awful, isn't it? I'm big as an elephant."

"You are not," Daniel insisted. As near to full-blood Choctaw as could be found, Daniel surprised Ivy by flushing hotly. Even the scalp beneath his ink-black hair seemed to glow a dark, dusky red. "It's what they call a high-pressure pregnancy, lots of fluid."

"All the more cushion for our little girl," Rose said, smiling down at her stomach.

Little girl.

Ivy's heart cracked open inside her chest, and the grief she'd kept bottled up for all these years poured out. Memories stormed her, yet she managed, just barely, to maintain a rigid calm.

"It's a girl," she heard the nurse say, cold metal gliding over her skin as the fuzzy, black-and-white image coalesced on the screen beside the examination table.

"It's a girl," the doctor announced months later, whisking the baby away.

A little girl, whom Ivy had never held or even seen, except at a distance.

A little girl who called someone else "Mommy."

Chapter Two

"My sister-in-law, Cara," Ryan said, standing in front of his chair. He'd stayed longer at Ivy's table than he'd intended, so long that his family had finally wandered over in search of him, necessitating a spate of introductions.

Ivy clapped her long slender hands to her cheeks, gaping at Cara. "I'm so sorry! I had no idea you were part of the Jefford family."

Ryan glanced from one to the other, surprised that they had evidently already met.

Cara laughed. "No reason why you should have known. I understand you haven't been around for a while, and the wedding was just three weeks ago. I should have made my identity clear when we met at the motel."

"I just never dreamed that Holt had married," Ivy said, exclaiming, "And you, too, Charlotte! It's been a season of weddings for the Jeffords."

Charlotte laughed. "So it has."

Ryan said, "I was telling Ivy about the house you and Ty are building."

"Yes, the old Moffat place, just east of here," Charlotte said, smiling that utterly content smile of hers.

"What a beautiful spot," Ivy murmured. "I've always loved that place."

"Listen, Cara's been on her feet all day," Holt interrupted, his arm curling around Cara's shoulders as he addressed his brother. "We're going to find our seats now."

Ryan nodded saying, "You go on. I'll be along shortly."

"I could use a chair myself," Ty announced, urging Charlotte to follow Holt.

"Nice to see you again, Ivy," Charlotte said, falling in line.

"You, too. And congratulations! Both of you. I mean, all of you!"

The family moved away with smiles and little waves. Ryan intended to say a quick goodbye and take his leave as well, but then Rose began to push up from the table, muttering that she should visit the ladies' room before dinner. Daniel stood to help her to her feet, and then trailed along behind her protectively, leaving Ryan alone with Ivy. Not only did it seem rude to walk away at that point, he found that he did not want to. Ivy had always intrigued him, and that appeared not to have changed. He glanced at his wristwatch and saw that he had about a quarter-hour before he must report to the head table, so he sat down again.

"You don't have to keep me company," Ivy said with a gentle smile.

"Nonsense," he told her. "We have lots to catch up on. So what have you been doing with yourself? Why haven't I seen you in all these years?"

Ivy's smile wilted around the edges and shadows darkened her warm brown eyes. "I've been on the move pretty much the whole time. That's how it is in my business. You go from one radio market to another, hoping to catch on in enough places to build a national following so you can squeeze a few more dollars out of the next contract."

To Ryan, that seemed a singularly unappealing way to live. He couldn't imagine pulling up roots every few months. "Where are you working now?"

"If all goes as planned, Oklahoma City."

"Ah, so that's what finally brings you our way."

She shrugged delicately. "It just all sort of worked out."

"Must be difficult to make friends and build relationships, moving around so much," he surmised. "I assume you're not married since I notice that you're unescorted and not wearing a ring." He reached for her left hand and turned it over atop the table as if to prove his point.

"I'm not married," she confirmed before looking pointedly at his own hand. "Neither, apparently, are you."

He laughed. "Never married. Never even been close."

"And here you've stayed all this time?"

"And here I've stayed all this time. Maybe that's the problem. There aren't many single women here in Eden."

"Oh, but there are many ways to meet people, surely. I mean, stranger things have happened."

"You're telling me! Just look at Holt and Charlotte."

"So why not you?" Ivy asked, her eyes locking with his.

"To tell you the truth, I think I'm just too busy. I don't have time to date, let alone fall in love and get married." He spread his hands, and smiled. "So what's your excuse?"

Ivy looked down, saying, "I drove a nail in that coffin a long time ago."

The forced lightness of her tone hinted at sadness, and Ryan suddenly felt ill at ease. Shifting in his seat, he strove to bring back a casual, chatty air. "Career girl, huh?"

"Something like that."

"I understand devotion to one's career, believe me," he said, sounding a little too hearty even to his own ears yet somehow unable to stop himself.

"Education is my calling, and let me tell you, it's more than a full-time job. Much as I love it, though, it gets in the way of normal life. Take your dad, for instance," he blundered on. "I'm ashamed to say I haven't seen him or even thought of him in a long time. Until I saw you here tonight, I didn't realize how long it's been."

"Really?" she asked, looking slightly stricken. "You haven't seen him *at all?*"

Ryan wanted to bite his tongue. Now she sounded worried.

"No, I'm sorry, not in…well, months, at least."

"Not even at church?"

"Not even at church," he confirmed.

"I'm assuming you still attend First Church," she said anxiously.

"Yes, I do, but—" He gulped. Where was a hole when he needed one? And why didn't she already know this? "Olie doesn't."

"He doesn't?"

"According to Holt, he goes with Rose and Daniel and their boys to our new sister church, Magnolia Christian."

Ivy seemed to ponder that. Gazing off into the distance, she murmured, "I see. Yes, I suppose that makes sense." She glanced back at Ryan, straightened, put on a smile again and said brightly, "I'm sure his grandsons decided that for him. Rose says he dotes on her two boys."

Disturbed, Ryan studied that smile and found that it did not quite reach her eyes. The Ivy that he glimpsed there in those cinnamon brown depths seemed once more sad, a little lost, uncertain. He had the urge to take her hand again, but didn't.

"I guess you'll all be attending Easter services at the Magnolia church together," he ventured cautiously.

Her chin lifted as if she would nod, but then she looked away again. After a moment, she haltingly told him, "I can't quite see myself attending Easter services anywhere but at First Church."

Ryan nodded, pleased and troubled at the same time. "That's good to hear. We'd love to have your family join us."

He caught the sharp edge of agony in her eyes and wondered what he'd said before her gaze skittered around the room. Suddenly, he understood that if Ivy attended First Church tomorrow, she would do so alone. Before he even knew what he intended, he heard himself saying, "N-naturally, Rose's family will want to be at their home church, so maybe you'd like to go with us. I mean, you're at the motel already, and—"

She stopped his flow of ill-considered words by grasping his sleeve lightly with her fingertips. "That's very sweet of you, Ryan, but not necessary."

The touch of her fingers cemented his resolve to keep her from attending Easter services alone.

"No, really. Since the weather's nice, we'll probably all just walk over from the motel together. Won't have to fight for a parking space that way. Why don't you come with me, er, with us?"

"Does First Church still do a sunrise Easter service in the park?" she asked.

Ryan nodded. "Granddad can't quite manage it anymore. Too much walking and standing."

"But they still do it?"

"Absolutely."

She sat back with a look of anticipation on her face. "Well, then, that's where I'll be."

"Maybe you wouldn't mind a little company," he suggested, surprising himself.

Ivy sat forward again, looking as surprised as he felt. After a moment, her warm, brown eyes began to glow. "Really?"

"It's a beautiful service, and I'd like to go. No reason we can't walk over together."

"That sounds lovely, Ryan."

Ryan was relieved to see that she meant it. The shadows he glimpsed behind her smile seemed to have fled.

He spied the Halseys returning then, Daniel following as Rose maneuvered her belly through the tables and chairs. He saw, too, that most people had taken their seats, and he knew the moment of his departure had come. Oddly reluctant to go, Ryan nevertheless got to his feet squeezing Ivy's hand once more as he said, "Shall I knock on your door, say half past six?"

"That sounds about right. It's number four, by the way."

"Number four. See you in the morning, then."

"I'm looking forward to it." Ivy smiled warmly. He flipped a wave at the Halseys and turned toward the dais, smoothing his tie with one hand.

What had he just done? Ryan wondered as he made his way to the front of the room. Escorting a single woman to a sunrise church service was one thing, but dealing with his family's questions about it would be something else. Then again, they didn't really have to know, did they? It would mean attending regular services later with the family, but two church services in one morning never did a fellow harm. That way, everyone would be happy. Ivy wouldn't have to go alone, he'd get to take part again in a service he truly enjoyed, the family would be together as usual, and that would be that. Satisfied with his plans, he turned his attention to enjoying the festivities.

The committee chairwoman beckoned to him, her smile looking a tad strained, and he put Ivy Villard out of his mind as best he could, focusing instead on his duties. That, after all, was what Ryan Jefford did best. Some might even have said that it defined him as a person, and he wouldn't have argued with them. It would not even have occurred to him to do so.

* * *

Ivy remained at her sister's side throughout the banquet. They'd had little time to talk as yet, but Ivy did not doubt that Rose was glad to see her, and for now that was enough. Ivy laughed at Ryan's witty welcome and sat patiently through the less entertaining speeches that followed, accompanied by a plate of unremarkable food served by girls in short-skirted, green-and-yellow uniforms emblazoned with the white Eden lightning bolt. Ivy remembered well doing the same thing, serving tables for tips on reunion night to raise funds for the cheer squad, and she had come prepared with a generous donation.

All in all her plan had thus far been even more successful than Ivy had hoped. Meeting Rose in a public place had been both more difficult and easier than Ivy had imagined. Rose had been shocked to see her, yes, but no more so than Ivy had been upon realizing that her sister was already the mother of two and expecting another child.

Rose's welcome had been all that Ivy could have asked for, warm, exuberant, even tearful, but the time and place of their reunion had relegated all but the simplest of exchanges to the future. Ivy sensed that Daniel might not be best pleased with her at the moment, but Ivy couldn't blame him. Had she realized Rose's physical condition beforehand, she would not have risked stressing her sister emotionally. That, too, however, was a subject for the future.

While her attention and intent centered on Rose, many of Ivy's old classmates had wandered by for a greeting and quick conversation. She'd been hugged and patted and smiled on. No one had surprised her as much as Ryan, though, and she silently thanked him for providing her with an easy out when Rose tentatively suggested that she join the family for Easter services the next day.

Rose interrupted her musings with the whispered invitation, "Daniel and I wonder if you'd like to join us for Easter tomorrow?"

"Oh sweetie, I'm sorry," Ivy replied softly, "but I've already promised to go to the services at First Church with Ryan Jefford. Besides, I don't think Dad would be very pleased."

Rather than press Ivy to reconsider, Rose's tawny brown eyes were suddenly alight with speculation. She leaned close to whisper, "With Ryan? Really? He's considered quite the catch around here, you know."

"We're just old friends, Rose," Ivy pointed out softly. "Mere acquaintances, really, but he invited me, and I said I would go."

Fortunately, before more could be said on the subject, the master of ceremonies, a retired former superintendent of Eden schools, announced that the highlight of the evening would commence. Each of the alumni present would stand and be recognized, in alphabetical order, while moderators read a list of his or her accomplishments. In this way, it was explained, they could all "catch up" with each other.

Ivy cringed at the idea and even considered pleading exhaustion or headache in order to slip out before her turn came. In the end, however, she did neither, reminding herself that turning over a new leaf meant putting away cowardly and dishonest habits once and for all. Besides, how much could anyone in Eden, other than her family, really know about her life? When the moderator at last called her name, Ivy stood and inwardly gulped as a paragraph taken directly from her personal promotional Web site was read.

"Ivy Villard has enjoyed a successful career in the highly competitive field of commercial radio. As half of the popular FireBrand Phillips and Ivy duo, she has logged thousands of on-air hours as an announcer, commentator and DJ, bringing her own special brand of humor, wit and organization to the new rock/talk format. As producer of the show, she has been instrumental in achieving the ratings that propelled it to the top of the heap. With the changing tastes of today's marketplace, however, the time has come to break up the act and branch out in different directions. Look for Ivy, a graduate of Southeastern Oklahoma State University with a degree in communications, at the helm of her own show in a market near you very soon."

The moderator went on to list awards that the show had won. Fan Favorite, Industry Pick, Top Market, Best New Format… Ivy closed her ears and barely heard the applause that followed. She couldn't help thinking that if the whole truth about Ivy Villard had been read, her reception would have been far less cordial. Clutching her sister's hand, Ivy dropped back into her chair and waited for the evening to be over.

Applauding for the umpteenth time, Ryan watched Ivy sit back down, one hand smoothing the seat of her chic black dress. He'd sensed her unease even before her name was called; then he'd caught the gossip being bandied about the head table.

"Have you ever listened to that show?" one of the women muttered.

"They say it's raunchy," another whispered, shaking her head.

"Disgraceful, I've heard," put in another.

Ryan squelched a spurt of disappointment. He disdained gossip of any kind, and he would not make judgments based on it, but in this case, if the rumors should be true, he would be very sad to hear it. Ivy could be considered little more than an acquaintance, really, even if he would be escorting her to sunrise service tomorrow, but he still hated to think that she might be involved in a show with a reputation for raunch.

He still wondered why he had offered to accompany her. If the service meant as much to her as it had seemed to earlier, he had nothing to worry about on her behalf. Except… Something was definitely going on behind those brown eyes. A blind man could have seen it. That troubled him as did his unexpected protective impulses where she seemed to be concerned.

Another name was read, and another alumni rose. Ryan shifted his attention to Garth White, class of 1970, owner of the largest independent insurance agency in Lawton. Garth hammed it up for the crowd, passing out business cards to those around him while the moderator cataloged his accomplishments, including record-breaking revenues, four sons and a number of grandsons. Ryan tried to pay attention, but his gaze kept straying back to Ivy. She looked poised and lovely, but he still could sense sorrow in her, a deep well of pain. He found himself wanting to walk over to her table again.

As he watched her, Ryan noticed a tall, painfully thin blonde in a short-sleeved, lilac print dress winding her way through the tables in a half crouch. When she reached Ivy's side, the two embraced warmly. Ivy pulled the blonde down onto the chair that Ryan had occupied earlier.

Ryan couldn't help wondering who the woman might be and what connection she had to Ivy. That the two were fond of each other was obvious. They clasped hands, whispering back and forth and exchanged grins. Ivy beamed, and for the first time since he'd laid eyes on her that evening, she seemed relaxed and happy. He watched as she whispered apparent introductions to her sister and brother-in-law while Cotton Carlson, the retired superintendent of schools, announced from the dais that door prizes would now be awarded.

The blonde stayed to chat with Ivy throughout the dispensing of such donated items as flower arrangements, a free alignment from Froggy's Gas & Tire, bottle openers that played a tune every time a top popped and a fifty-dollar gift certificate from Booker's Grocery Emporium. When the program finally ended, Ryan rose to shake a few more hands and greet a few more familiar faces, while Ivy and her companions melted into the crush.

The crowd had begun to thin by the time Ryan came across his old buddy Matthew Barston. An algebra and Spanish teacher, Matt had worked for years at the small school district in Hilltown, a neighboring community some dozen or so miles to the east.

"Matt! I didn't know you were here. Why wasn't your name called tonight?"

Matthew flushed as red as his copper hair and shoved the hand that Ryan had just gripped into the pocket of his tweedy brown jacket. He cleared his throat before saying, "I asked them not to read my name. Call me odd, but I prefer not to stand up and have it announced that I'm out of a job."

Startled, Ryan seized his friend by the arm, demanding, "How could this happen? When did it happen?"

"As to when," Matt said, snorting with disgust, "Monday morning, less than forty-eight hours after I got married."

"Married!" Ryan exclaimed. There seemed to be a wedding epidemic going around.

"*Why* I'm out of a job is the real issue, though, isn't it?" Matt went on, grumbling, "Sanctimonious snobs."

Just then the skinny blonde Ryan had noticed at Ivy's table came into view, halting at Matt's side. Matt immediately straightened and slid an arm around her waist, his smile wiping all traces of anger from his face.

"Honey, this is my buddy Ryan Jefford, I've told you about him. Ryan, my wife, Devony."

Devony Barston's beautiful smile brightened her otherwise rather plain face, and her enormous green eyes regarded Ryan with warmth. "It's so nice to meet you. Matt has told me what a good friend you are."

Surprised, since he and Matt didn't talk all that much anymore or see each other outside of work but a few times a year, Ryan just nodded and smiled.

Matt gave Devony a squeeze and said, "Honey,

could you give us another minute? Won't take long, I promise."

"Sure." Devony smiled again, nodded at Ryan and moved away.

Ryan realized that he should have told Devony congratulations on their marriage, but it was too late for that.

"Sorry," he muttered to Matt. "I seem to be a step behind. Congratulations on your marriage. Please give my best wishes to your wife."

"Thanks. I hope you'll still feel that way after I ask you a favor."

"Well, sure, Matt," Ryan answered readily, "anything I can do."

"I'm getting ready to look for another job. Will you write me a recommendation?"

Ryan opened his mouth, then shut it again before carefully saying, "My impulse is to give you a flat yes, but I make it a policy to pray over every decision." That happened to be absolutely true, as far as it went, but said nothing to the fact that Ryan sensed more to Matt's story than his friend had revealed.

Matt ducked his head. "Sure. I understand."

"Give me a call in a few days," Ryan went on with a smile. He didn't have the faintest idea what had happened, whether Matt had been let go or why Matt should ask him for a recommendation; he only knew that he needed more information before he committed himself. On the one hand, Ryan could not imagine that Matt had done anything to get himself fired. On the other hand, this was not the time of year when normal budgetary constraints would dictate layoffs. A clash of personalities perhaps? He prayed that it wasn't something worse. Educators, after all, held positions open to public censure. Christian educators, especially, should aim to be above reproach.

Ryan watched with a heavy heart as Matt walked away. *What a rotten break*, Ryan thought, *just married and out of a job*. He bowed his head to say a quick prayer for his friend. A moment later, he found himself scanning the room for Ivy. How, he wondered, did she know the new Mrs. Matthew Barston? And why had Ivy's eyes been shadowed with pain?

Chapter Three

Night still blanketed the town when Ryan knocked on the door of Ivy's room early the next morning. He hunched his shoulders beneath the nubbly, caramel-tan fabric of his sport coat. The jacket, worn with a pale yellow shirt, dark brown slacks and a patterned tie in rich tones of gold, provided little comfort from the early morning chill, but he trusted that the temperature would soon warm.

The door opened to reveal Ivy in a pale pink knit sheath with fitted, three-quarter-length sleeves and a straight neckline. Her dark, lustrous hair hung straight down her back.

"Hello," she said, smiling broadly. The warmth of her welcome went a long way toward wiping out Ryan's nebulous regret at having offered to escort her this morning. He was too busy to get involved with anyone, no matter how much he liked Ivy.

"You're looking very pretty," he told her truthfully, "especially for such an early hour."

"Why, thank you. You're turned out quite nicely yourself."

He tugged on the cuffs and lapels of his jacket, preening comically and enjoying her laughter. She interrupted his performance by asking, "Do I need a coat?"

"Something light, I'd think. It's not cold but still a little cool out."

Ivy went to the suitcase atop the nondescript dresser, picked up a silky, oversized shawl in a pastel paisley print and tossed it about her shoulders. "Will this do?"

"Perfect," Ryan decreed. "You look like a spring morning."

Laughing again, Ivy retrieved the key and stepped down out of the comfortable room, pulling the door closed behind her. She locked the door and handed the key to Ryan, saying, "I don't have any pockets and would prefer to leave my purse here. Would you mind holding this for me?"

"No problem." Palming the key and the hard plastic tag attached to it, he slid his hand into his coat pocket, then ushered her along the row of rooms, each one separated from the next by a parking bay open on one end. Her perfume wafted on the still, cool air, a combination of spicy cinnamon and sweet camellia well matched to the woman who wore it.

The barest glimmer of light showed in the east as they strolled along, side by side. Ahead, Ryan could make out cars jockeying for parking space and people moving about; yet, despite that, a certain expectant stillness lay over the place.

"Hard to believe we were socked in with a nasty ice storm just a month and a half ago," he ventured after several moments.

"Yeah, we got hit up in Tulsa, too," she said, "but then that area almost always gets it. You guys down here not so much."

"Usually once a year," he noted, "and this year it got us really good."

"Holt and Cara must have been in a panic, with the wedding coming up and all," Ivy commented idly.

Ryan chuckled. "Nope. Nobody was thinking wedding then. Well, Holt and Cara weren't. The rest of us could read the writing on the wall. I have to hand it to them, though, once the idea hit, they didn't waste any time. Almost before we knew it, we were standing up there in front of the altar watching them do the deed."

Ivy shook her head. "Maybe that's how it has to be sometimes," she mused, "fast and furious. What's that old saying? 'Don't let the grass grow under your feet'?"

"No danger of that," Ryan quipped. "We're already expecting to hear any day that they are expecting."

A tiny gasp escaped Ivy. "So soon?"

"Why not?" Ryan asked. "Ace, Cara's little boy, is just a year old, but chances are he'd be at least two before Cara could give him a brother or sister, and as Holt points out, they would like them to be close in age—similar to the two years between Holt and me."

"What about Ace's father?" Ivy asked carefully.

"He died not long after Ace was born."

She hunched her shoulders, drawing her wrap tighter. "How sad."

"Yes. Yes, it is." Ryan didn't say that from the sound of things, the marriage hadn't been a very good one or that Ace's natural father had looked on him as more of a means to extract cash from his own parents than as a treasured son.

They walked on in silence for a few moments. Dawn hovered over the horizon now, ready to illuminate the city with the softest tendrils of day and outline the still-leafless skeletons of the stately pecan and hickory trees. It felt as if the world waited for the dawning of the Easter sun.

"I'd forgotten that sound," Ivy said suddenly.

"What's that?"

"The oil pumps."

"Yeah," Ryan lifted his head to catch the rhythmic *ka-shunk, ka-shunk*. "I never notice it. Unless it's *not* there. And one day it won't be. They're gradually replacing these old pumps with a quiet electric system."

"That's too bad," she said wistfully. "I find it a comforting sound."

"Yeah, I guess I do, too. It nearly drove Ty crazy at first," Ryan divulged with a chuckle. "Turns out that a penthouse is a very quiet atmosphere."

"How did Charlotte and Tyler Aldrich ever get together?" Ivy asked, looking up at Ryan.

Suddenly struck by the elegant perfection of her features—delicate chin and brows, high smooth forehead, large, deeply set eyes of warm reddish brown, glossy pink lips bracketed by the most beguiling dimples, and a straight, slender nose—he couldn't respond for a moment. Then a memory intruded, one he hadn't even known he'd locked away, and before he could think better of it, he heard himself blurting it out.

"Wait a minute. Didn't you used to have a little bump on the bridge of your nose?"

Ivy lifted a hand to that spot on her face, patches of dusky red blossoming on the apples of her cheeks. "You aren't supposed to know that!"

"You did," Ryan teased. "You had a cute little bump right at the top of the bridge of your nose."

Dropping her hand, she grimaced. "Cute stops being cute at about twenty-four, thank you very much."

"So you had it removed."

"Yes, if you must know, I had it removed."

Grinning, Ryan couldn't resist the urge to tease her a little more. "You were the envy of every girl in town back in high school, and all along I'd bet you were obsessing about that tiny bump."

"I didn't," she insisted. "Well, maybe a little bit, but it was my boyfriend who insisted I do it." Abruptly, she snapped her mouth closed, as if regretting that last part. Ryan felt a pang on her behalf.

"What a jerk," he declared.

"You don't know the half of it," she muttered darkly.

Again, a question fell out of his mouth without routing itself through his brain first. "How'd you wind up with a jerk like that?"

She sent an elbow to his ribs, just hard enough to make him laugh. "Basically, the same way I wound up here with you," she retorted. "Now, enough about me. We were talking about Charlotte and Tyler Aldrich."

"Right. Charlotte and Ty and how they got together." Ryan cleared his throat of his laughter. "Simple really. Ty got stranded here overnight back in the fall. One night became a week. Later, his visits pretty much became dates. The next thing we knew, they couldn't live without each other. You know how it goes. Now they're building a big new house here and hoping that our grandfather, Hap, will move in with them once it's finished."

"Is that likely?"

Ryan sucked in a deep breath, mentally shifting gears. "I'm not sure he'll have any other choice in the end. He's almost eighty-one, and his arthritis isn't going to get any better. If not for Cara, he couldn't manage the motel now."

"And if she has a new baby, she won't be able to help out," Ivy concluded.

"Exactly. I can't see Holt letting her continue much longer in any event," Ryan mused aloud. "Quite the protector, our Holt. Can't say I blame him, though. It's physically demanding work, and as you know, Cara's a little thing."

"What will happen to the motel if your grandfather gives it up?" Ivy asked.

"Ty and Charlotte have a young Hispanic couple they'd like to bring in to take over, with an eye maybe to buying the place. Makes sense when you think about it. None of us is going to take on the place. But, as I said, it's Hap's decision."

"Will he be unreasonable?"

"No, I don't think so. That's not Granddad. In the end, I think he'll give it up for the great-grandbabies."

"Babies? Plural?"

Ryan shrugged. "Holt and Cara make no secret of their intentions, and Charlotte and Ty will start a family eventually, I'm sure. Probably sooner rather than later. And there's Ace, already."

"Hap accepts him as part of the family?"

"Of course. We all do."

Ivy turned a look up at him that seemed part hope and part doubt. "Just like that?"

Ryan chuckled. "You obviously haven't met my nephew yet. He's quite the little charmer."

"Actually," Ivy said, ducking her head, "I think I have. He seems to have that confidence peculiar to children who are greatly loved."

"You bet. That's what babies are for, isn't it? Loving?"

She didn't answer that. After a moment, Ryan felt compelled to ask, "What about you? You interested in having children some day?"

Ivy tucked her chin to her chest. "I don't think I'm meant for that."

"Well, that makes two of us," he said, needing, for some reason, to validate her choice.

Her head popped up. "Really? You don't want a family of your own?" She sounded affronted, yet she'd just basically said the same thing, hadn't she?

"The way I look at it," Ryan explained carefully, "I already have a family, a suddenly growing family, and of course I have my students."

"They must mean a lot to you."

He smiled. "Can't seem to help it. You might even say the thing's gotten a bit out of hand. Some of them really need an adult to just listen."

Ivy tilted her head, the sleek curtain of her long dark hair sweeping across her shoulder blades. "Is that enough for you? Listening to other people's kids?"

Ryan shifted uncomfortably. "Well…my job and my family keep me very busy, and…" He rubbed a hand over his face before abruptly deciding to give in to the impulse to say what he had never said to anyone else. "You probably remember what happened when my dad died."

"Your mom's suicide," Ivy whispered, nodding.

"Marriage seems like a really big risk to me," he admitted.

"I used to think so, too."

"Not anymore?"

She pondered that before shrugging. "I don't know," she said softly. "Love is risky, no doubt about it, but family…" She looked up at him with wide, pain-filled eyes. "Family is worth very nearly everything."

She had a point there, Ryan admitted silently. He would risk much for his family, not just Hap and Holt and Charlotte, but for his brother-in-law and sister-in-law and nephew, too. What would he risk for a wife and child of his own? He was almost afraid to find out.

"Quite a crowd this year," Ryan remarked softly, looking around at the people already spread over the gently rolling landscape.

Ivy nodded in agreement. There were more people present than she remembered from years past, but it had been so long that she had no idea if this had become the norm.

The simple service of yesteryear had obviously given way to a more sophisticated approach. She noticed an outdoor sound system tucked into inconspicuous places, and flickering patio torches had been placed at intervals to mark the space from which the service would be conducted. Atop the hill behind that space, in increasingly stark silhouette, stood three crosses temporarily erected for the service. Around the topmost section of the center cross hung a crown fashioned of thorny vines.

In the center of the marked-off space stood a large rock, across which a length of purple fabric and several long-stemmed lilies had been arranged in artful abandon. This apparently served as a makeshift altar as two men knelt next to it in fervent prayer. One of them she recognized as Grover Waller, the middle-aged pastor of First Church, a little older and rounder and with thinner hair, but the same pastor nonetheless. The other was a younger man Ivy did not know. At her whispered query, Ryan informed her that his name was Davis Latimer, the new minister of the church on Magnolia. He, along with his congregation, had been invited to participate in this earliest Easter morning service.

Ivy felt a chill. Glancing around, she wondered if her father might be in attendance. She looked down, telling herself that if he saw her he would surely avoid her. Perhaps it would be best if he did see her. It would spare Rose the awkwardness of having to inform him of her visit.

A reverent hush enveloped the ever-growing crowd, some of whom stood or crouched. Others had possessed the foresight to bring along lawn chairs, while still others simply sat or knelt on the ground.

"I should have thought to bring something to sit on," Ryan told her apologetically, leaning close.

Ivy gripped the sides of her wrap and held them out. "This will do."

"Won't you be chilled without it?"

"We'll find a sheltered spot that blocks the breeze."

"Let's try over here," he suggested, taking her hand to lead her down the gentle slope a little way to a cluster of boxy shrubs. Ivy spread the paisley shawl on the ground in front of the shrubs and sat, folding her legs back to one side. Ryan followed suit, scooting close to offer her the warmth of his large, muscular body, one palm braced flat on the ground behind her. "Comfortable?"

"Yes, thank you."

They sat in silence for several minutes, watching the gradual lightening of the sky, before the pastors stood, Bibles in hand, and took up positions in front of the makeshift altar. Utter stillness descended, then Grover opened his Bible and in a clear but gentle voice began to read the prayer of

Jesus from the seventeenth chapter of *John.* The other man picked up with the eighteenth and nineteenth chapters, telling about the betrayal and arrest of Christ, which included the Apostle John's moving account of the crucifixion, before Grover began the twentieth.

"Now on the first day of the week Mary Magdalene came early to the tomb, while it was still dark, and saw the stone already taken away from the tomb…."

The pastor went on as the sun rose over the hilltop behind him, its golden rays seeming to reach out to all the world. He read how the risen Savior showed Himself to His astonished, jubilant followers and became the Light that pierces the darkness. Finally, Grover closed his Bible and stepped forward to speak.

"Mocked, stripped, scourged until His flesh hung in strips and, finally, in the company of murderers and thieves, nailed by the hands and feet to a cross," the preacher began. "That is the picture that His enemies would have had you remember, but they did not recognize what was really happening, what they themselves were a part of. They did not see a willing sacrifice, a life laid down in recompense for the sins of humanity or a love so great that it could allow such a thing. And they were not there when Christ took up His earthly form once more and stood among His beloved, proving

Himself to be the Son of God, worthy and perfect in every way. So today, as we, His children, bask in the radiance of His resurrection, grow in the glow of His love and rejoice in the light of the forgiveness and grace with which He gifted us, let us praise Him."

Lifting their hands, the pastors began to pray, one after the other praising and thanking God with simple eloquence and humble gratitude. At the end, they spoke a gentle "Amen" together, which the congregation echoed. Then a woman whom Ivy recognized as former classmate Becca Inman stood in the midst of the crowd and began to sing a well-known Easter hymn in a clear, beautiful voice. Others began to join in, coming to their feet as they did so. With the song gaining in volume, Ivy, with Ryan at her side, also rose.

She did not realize that tears streamed down her face until Ryan pressed a clean linen handkerchief into her hand. With her thoughts elsewhere, she barely managed a smile for him. Instead, she envisioned that glorious day of resurrection. That miraculous event proved the sacrificial intent of the crucifixion, but for so long Ivy had ignored it, seeing it as just one more improbable, two-thousand-year-old story that had nothing to do with her own life today.

Ivy knew now what a fool she had been. She'd looked at her father, a man who had always gone to church, and seen the bitterness that had marked his life. She'd wanted no part of that, and somehow that bitterness had equated with church in her mind, and church had equated with Christ. Only when she'd been introduced to her Savior and surrendered her life to Him had the stories of Easter become dear to her, more dear than all she had given up to follow her Lord.

She had found forgiveness and a new beginning by surrendering her heart and soul to Jesus Christ. In many ways, she felt resurrected herself. But sin, as she had learned, still has consequences. She understood that, like everyone else, she lived with the consequences of her choices in the here and now. Thankfully, she could trust God to give her everything she needed to cope with those consequences. He would help her stop making the mistakes that had so devastated her life.

Ivy closed her eyes and claimed that promise again now. *Dear Lord, show me how to live to please You, and help me make up for all I've done. Help me mend what I've broken and ease the pain I've caused. Help me endure the anguish I've caused myself and find some measure of peace. Most of all, show me Your will for my life, and help me to live it. Thank You for Your Son and His sacrifice. Thank You for Your forgiveness and for choosing to see me through Him. Amen.*

She felt a moment, an instant, of that longed-for

peace. Then, suddenly, there came a shift in the atmosphere, a literal tightening of the air around her, like the moment before a lightning strike. Ivy opened her eyes to encounter the angry visage of her father. Stunned, she could do no more than stare back at first.

He looked worn and tired, far older than his fifty-four years. The skin of his long, narrow face drooped in loose wrinkles, while gray streaks roughened the thatch of his light brown hair and liberally salted his bushy eyebrows, giving him the hangdog expression of a man who had seen and lost too much. As her heart lurched into her throat, Ivy's conscience cried out, *I did that to him!* Thankfully, the words did not make it to her mouth. Ryan spoke first.

"Hello, Olie. I was just telling Ivy last night how long it's been since I saw you."

Her father ignored Ryan, his icy, gray glare burning into her like the flames of the still-flickering torches. Ivy glanced around, realized that the service had ended and took a tentative step closer, saying urgently, "Dad, I—I didn't expect to see you here."

"Me?" he mocked. "*You* didn't expect to see *me* here?" He stabbed a finger at the ground, declaring, "This is my home, girl, not yours, not anymore. I thought I made that plain when you showed up the last time!"

"Dad, please," she begged softly, all too aware

of Ryan standing there. "That was a long time ago. I know I disappointed you. I disappointed myself, and I've paid a heavy price for it. Can't we at least talk about it?"

"Talk?" he scoffed. "Not likely."

"I just want to tell you how sorry I am, Daddy."

"Don't call me that! I'm not your daddy. No tramp like you will ever be a daughter of mine."

"Olie!" Ryan exclaimed, his tone that of the scolding assistant principal.

"You don't know the truth about her," Olie told him roughly. "No one does, because I've kept her secrets." He shook a finger at her. "But only so long as she stayed away. Now she's here, the truth will finally come out, and the truth is she sleeps with a man she never married and makes her living spreading filth. She even got herself—"

"Please don't!" Ivy cried, interrupting him before he could spew the worst of it. "Please! I've changed."

"Change?" Olie ridiculed. "It's too late for change! Just go slither back under your rock and leave us be!"

Ivy couldn't bear anymore. Clutching Ryan's arm, she stammered an incoherent apology.

"S-So sorry. I—I never thought he'd be here. Excuse me! I—I need..." She took off at a run, fresh tears streaming down her face.

Behind her, she heard Ryan speaking in his stern, assistant principal's voice, but she didn't even try to register the words. What did it matter anyway? What did any of it matter? Her father would never forgive her, never let her forget, even for a moment, what she'd done. As if she could!

Ignoring the curious stares of others, she hurried away, wanting only to reach the privacy of her room, where she could pour out her heart to God and see if she could recapture even a glimmer of the peace she so desperately wanted.

Chapter Four

Ryan parked his hands at his waist, watching in shock as Ivy fled the park in tears. Turning back to the author of this ugly public scene, he pinned Olie Villard in place with a glare before stepping close to growl, "Good grief, man! What's wrong with you?"

Even slightly cowed, Olie remained unrepentant, sticking out his long, narrow chin at a pugnacious angle. "*She's* what's wrong with me, Ivy and her filthy ways. Like mother, like daughter, I tell you, and if you're smart you'll keep your distance from her!" Swinging his lanky frame around, he stalked away, his hands fisted at his sides.

Sighing, Ryan cast a wary glance over the area, wondering who might have overheard. He saw several curious onlookers but turned aside their attention with a level gaze and pointed smile before bending to sweep up the shawl that Ivy had left behind in her haste. He shook out the thing, telling himself that he would return it. Frowning, he considered Olie's unpleasant words and Ivy's tearful response.

She hadn't exactly denied her father's accusations or, in all fairness, admitted to them. Still, at this point, Ryan could not escape the unhappy conclusion that Ivy had made some big mistakes in her life.

He was not one to judge; he'd made his own blunders. After the deaths of his parents, Ryan had figured that he had no reason to live an exemplary life. Why should he live his life, according to the godly rules and ethics taught him by his father and grandparents? What good had it done his dad?

His mother had always been rather fragile. The only child of a doting, widowed, older father, she'd been too well protected in many ways and more than a little self-centered. When her husband had died so unexpectedly in a freak accident on the job, her chief concern had been who would take care of her with him gone? No one had realized until it was too late, that in her grief and panic, she would swallow every prescription pill she could find.

As a college student separated from his remaining family by just enough distance to guarantee no interference from them, Ryan had buried his grief and anger with months of partying. He had told himself at the time that it was nothing more than a rite of passage. Only after returning home for the summer and reconnecting with his older brother, younger sister and paternal grandparents did he find enough peace to reclaim God's purpose for his life.

The rest of the family had been struggling, too, but together they had all managed to put the dual tragedy behind them. In helping to assuage their pain, Ryan had found balm for his own. The steady, sturdy love of his family had given him strength and direction, and their wise counsel had helped him find his calling. He'd learned to value the integrity of his own soul above gold or anything else the world had to offer.

He knew too well how easily rebellion could be justified by a spirit blinded with grief or rage or the lure of worldly things, so he would not judge Ivy. Getting caught up in a public family feud made him distinctly uncomfortable, and he certainly wasn't ready to upset the order of his life, no matter how drawn he felt to the beautiful woman Ivy had become. Still, he could not help wanting to protect Ivy from her father's anger.

He would return the shawl, but perhaps, Ryan decided, it would be best to give Ivy some time alone. Maybe, in the meantime, he could figure out the best way to deal with this mess. Her wrap in hand, he trudged back to the motel to seek the counsel of his family. So much for his intention to keep them in the dark concerning his date, if that was the word for it, with Ivy this morning. Along the way back to the motel, he prayed for guidance, knowing that if he was not very careful he could find himself more involved than seemed wise for a man who had never been comfortable with the idea of trusting his heart to any woman.

"I admit I heard some talk about Ivy," Hap Jefford said in his gravelly voice, "and I been concerned for some time now 'bout Olie."

Dropping down into his usual chair at one end of the oval maple dining table in the apartment behind the lobby of the motel, Hap bent and began the process of lacing up his boots with fingers gnarled by age and arthritis.

"Carrying around that much bitterness can't be good for a fellow," Holt put in, turning away from the high chair where he had just deposited Ace. Going down on his haunches, he began to help his grandfather with the boots.

The two so resembled each other, despite the forty-four years between them, that old photos of Hap were often mistaken for current ones of Holt.

The family had just returned from the late service at First Church, and while Charlotte and Cara had gone into the small kitchen to get dinner on the table, the men had made themselves comfortable in the apartment dining room. For Holt, Ty and Ryan, that amounted to removing their jackets and ties and rolling up their shirtsleeves before taking their customary chairs at the table; for Hap it meant shucking his decades-old black suit and trading it for his usual flannel shirt, denim overalls and work boots. Emerging from his bedroom once more, he had picked up the conversation about Ivy where they'd left off earlier.

"Care to elaborate on just what it is that you've heard?" Ryan asked. Much as he disliked gossip, he wanted to know what caused Ivy's pain and Olie's anger.

Hap shrugged and rasped, "Mostly it was about that radio show of hers. I've heard the term *vulgar* in connection with it."

That, unfortunately, dovetailed with what Ryan had heard at the banquet the previous night.

"I've listened to that show," Ty admitted. "I'm ashamed to say it used to be one of my favorites. For what it's worth, it was mostly her partner, Fire-Brand Phillips, saying and doing the risqué things, but vulgar isn't too strong a term for what I heard. I guess the thing is that when being outrageous is your trademark, you have to find a way to constantly outdo yourself. It got to be too much for me even before I met the Lord."

Hap made a mournful, disapproving sound deep in his throat. "Pitiful way to make a living."

Ace growled in an attempt to copy the old man's sound, and Hap smiled indulgently at the boy. Theirs was a mutual admiration society.

Charlotte came in from the kitchen bearing china dishes and flatware, which she carried to the table before heading over to the maple hutch to gather tablecloth, place mats and napkins. "According to what they said when they recognized her at the banquet last night," Charlotte reminded them, "that's all behind Ivy now. She and that Phillips have broken up the act."

"That is what it sounded like," Holt agreed.

"Look, for all we know, Ivy had a change of heart about the way she was making her living," Charlotte said. "I, for one, think she should get the benefit of the doubt."

"She did go to early service with Ryan this morning," Holt pointed out.

"Which had nothing, I'm sure, to do with him personally," Ty quipped, "him being such an unappealing cuss."

Ryan pulled a face at his brother-in-law. "I don't think she'd have gone at all if she'd known Olie would be there."

"Shame, what he did," Hap said.

"She ran off in tears," Ryan recalled softly. "It was heartbreaking."

"Even if what the gossips say about Ivy is true," Charlotte went on, "Christians should show her the love of Christ, as I'm sure you all know."

"Well, that settles it then," Hap announced, slapping a knee for emphasis.

Ace smacked the tray of his high chair.

"Settles what?" Ryan asked in confusion, unaware of anything that needed to be settled.

"We're inviting her to dinner, that's what," Charlotte answered briskly. Charlotte had been thirteen when their parents had died and, with both of her older brothers out on their own, she'd moved into the motel with their grandparents. At twenty-seven, having lived more than half her life with Hap Jefford, she could practically read the old man's mind. Charlotte and their grandfather had grown especially close after the death of their grandmother a few years ago, so close that her brothers had feared she would devote herself to Hap and never marry.

"You've got to take her key over anyway," Cara told Ryan from the kitchen doorway, an apron cinched around her slender waist. "That's what she said when I let her in the room earlier, that you were holding her key for her and she'd forgotten to get it back."

That and the shawl, Ryan reflected unhappily. Shifting in his chair, he pressed his elbows to the tabletop and spread his hands, saying, "I'm not sure I'm the one who ought to speak to her."

"Of course you are," Charlotte retorted dismissively. "Who else?"

"Maybe she'd rather have a woman to talk to," he suggested hopefully.

"Instead of a strong shoulder to cry on?" Cara asked in a skeptical tone. "I don't think so."

Exasperated, Ryan sighed, knowing he was on the hook but still squirming. "Well, she might need a little more time to compose herself."

"Nothing raises the hair on the back of a man's neck like a woman's tears," Holt observed wisely, "because he's either got to run or let her use his shoulder for a hanky."

"Running would be cowardly," Charlotte sniffed.

"And the other doesn't sound very heroic, either, put that way," Cara chided lightly.

Holt lifted his eyebrows. "That's because you're not a man, thank the sweet Lord." That won him a warm smile and the glint of a promise from his wife's big, worshipful eyes. He smirked at Ryan. "Coward or hero? Your choice, little brother."

"Maybe because you're so experienced, you should do it," Ryan snapped.

Cara waved a hand to let them know she would be making that decision. "Uh. No." With that, she turned and disappeared into the kitchen, leaving a smugly grinning Holt behind her.

Ty cupped his hands behind his head and looked at Charlotte, who snorted and said, "Don't even think about it."

Ty turned to Ryan. "Sorry, pal. It's you or Hap."

"You took her to sunrise service," Hap grated out.

Rolling his eyes, Ryan pushed up to his feet,

snagged his coat from the back of his chair and tossed it on. Obviously, he would get no peace until he'd done what they wanted. Why had he wanted their advice, anyway?

"Just for that," he scolded, wagging his finger between his brother and brother-in-law, "you two can set the table without my help."

"Yes, sir, Mr. Jefford, sir," Tyler quipped, winking at Holt. "He does love that mantle of authority, doesn't he?" Holt chuckled.

Ace put back his head and laughed, not having the least idea what might be funny.

Ryan didn't dignify their laughter with a reply, but it was clear that no one here gave one instant's consideration to his discomfort. Didn't they realize that a small-town assistant principal and coach lived in a fishbowl? He couldn't be caught in the middle of a public family dispute—even if it wasn't *his* family.

"I'll get an extra place setting," Charlotte announced as Ryan turned toward the front room, adjusting his collar. "Way this family's growing," she went on, "we're going to have to buy more china soon."

Shaking his head, Ryan gathered up the paisley shawl and went out into the lobby, pulling the door closed behind him. Once alone, however, he paused to close his eyes and send up a quick prayer. He felt mixed emotions—guilt about his reluctance to face Ivy, yet a growing excitement at seeing her again.

Lord, I've always liked Ivy, and I can't help feeling sorry for her. I'll help her if I can, but please don't let me get sucked into something that I have no business getting involved in. I saw the hurt on her face and felt the sting of Olie's words, and I know that she needs comfort and support. I want to be her friend, I really do. And yes, I have to admit she's beautiful. Just show me how to help her without... He bowed his head a little lower, suddenly feeling chastised, and went on. *Just show me how to do it in a way that honors You. Amen.*

Couldn't go wrong with that, he told himself, patting his pocket to be sure the key hadn't gone missing and heading for Ivy's room.

This had to stop, Ivy told herself, sighing. She'd put it out of her mind for fifteen or twenty minutes, then she'd think of the look of contempt on her father's face, of the acid tone of his voice, and the pain would return. Feeling so hurt was stupid, because she'd expected him to react as he had. She wouldn't have believed it if he'd acted any other way. Still, it felt as if her heart had been cut out and handed to her on a platter, and all she seemed able to do, besides cry, was pray for strength.

Squaring her shoulders, she faced her image in the mirror over the dresser and took several deep breaths. She was in the midst of giving herself a stern, mental talking-to when the telephone beside the bed rang.

She'd noticed as soon as she'd arrived that her cell phone didn't have reception, and she hadn't made any calls from the room, so she couldn't imagine who besides her sister would be calling her. It wouldn't have been difficult, of course, for anyone who knew that she had taken a room at Heavenly Arms to reach her. Warily, she walked across the industrial-style carpeting and lifted the old-fashioned, corded receiver.

"Hello?"

"Hi, it's Rose."

Ivy smiled tremulously. "I thought it might be. Couldn't imagine who else would be calling me here."

"How was the sunrise service?"

Ivy sighed. "The service itself was lovely. What happened afterward..." She went on to glumly explain the confrontation with their father.

"I'm so sorry, Ivy," Rose said. "I didn't get a chance to tell him that you're in town."

"It's not your fault," Ivy told her sister. "I blindsided you, and now I've blindsided him, but it wasn't my intention. I went to the sunrise service in the first place because I thought Dad would be attending church with you guys."

"We thought so, too, but he didn't show up, and now I guess I know why."

"I hope I haven't caused trouble for you," Ivy said worriedly. "I first thought that you could mention you'd run into me at the reunion, sort of prepare him for meeting me face-to-face, but that was before I realized your condition."

Rose laughed at that. "I'm pregnant, sis. That's hardly a debilitating condition. I had every intention of telling Dad over dinner today that you're in town, but because he missed church, I doubt he'll show up for dinner, which is why I'm calling. Why don't you come over, meet the boys and have Easter dinner with us?"

Meet the boys. Rose's two sons would be under six years of age because neither had been born the last time Ivy had seen her sister. Rose hadn't even been noticeably pregnant. Then again, neither had Ivy. Noticeably, that was.

Ivy bit her lip, tears threatening once more at the thought of her daughter. Funny how she'd been able to put that pain away for a while, and now suddenly it was like being flayed alive every time she thought about Chelsea. Ivy knew that she was in no shape to meet her nephews at the moment. Gulping, she tried to keep her voice even.

"I'm sorry, Rose, but n-not today. Dad might still show up, and I'm afraid I've developed a killer headache since our run-in this morning. I'm just going to hang out here today. We'll talk again tomorrow morning and arrange something then."

Rose sighed. "I understand. But tomorrow, okay? Scott and Hunter are anxious to meet their Aunt Ivy."

Not as anxious as their Aunt Ivy was to *avoid* meeting them, Ivy told herself, pinching the bridge of her nose. She just didn't know if she could bear meeting Rose's children.

For the first time, she wondered if she'd made a horrible mistake in coming here. A knock at her door saved her from having to pursue either that idea or the conversation any further.

"Rose, someone's at my door. I'll call you in the morning. Thanks for the invitation. Bye."

Rose reluctantly let her go. Ivy placed the receiver in the cradle of the phone, calling out, "One moment!"

Rushing back to the mirror, Ivy sniffed and smoothed her hair. Nothing she could do would lessen the redness in the tip of her nose, however. Accepting that fact, she took the time to straighten the hem of the baggy, dark blue T-shirt that she wore with a comfortable pair of faded jeans before heading to the door. After one more deep breath, she reached for the knob.

For the second time that day, Ryan stood smiling at Ivy's door. This time, however, no answering smile lit her face. Instead, the gaze from her red-rimmed eyes barely touched on his before sliding away. Obviously embarrassed about what had happened that morning, she folded her arms in a protective posture. He said the first thing that popped into his mind.

"You okay?"

She nodded, but he saw her swallow and cleared his throat in sympathy.

"We, um, thought you might like to join us for dinner." Ivy bowed her head, prompting him to add, "Charlotte and Cara together lay as fine a table as you'll find anywhere." She took a breath, and he rushed on. "There's always plenty."

Sighing, she lifted a hand to her head and said, "I'm sorry, but I have a terrible headache just now."

He didn't doubt it a bit. Still, he hated to think of her weeping alone in her room. "You've got to eat."

She shook her head, muttering, "I'm not hungry."

"Aw, come on," he urged. "It's just the family. What can it hurt?"

"I'm not hungry!" she snapped. The next instant she squeezed her eyes closed and softened her tone. "Sorry. I—I just can't think of food right now. I'll get something later."

He didn't point out that there would be nothing to get later. Neither the diner downtown nor Booker's Grocery Emporium opened on Sundays, and the catfish joint outside of town would close after the midday rush, as it always did on Sundays.

Realizing then that he hadn't yet delivered her shawl and key, he hurried to rectify that oversight. "Oh. Uh." He lifted the hand with which he grasped her shawl and dug into his coat pocket with the other. "I almost forgot. You left these."

Gingerly she took the silky wrap from his hand and draped it over her arm then reached for the key. “Thank you. I’m afraid I wasn’t…that is, I…” She took a deep breath and finally met his gaze with hers. “I owe you an apology for what happened this morning.”

“That wasn’t your fault,” he said quietly, but she seemed intent on explaining.

“From what you said last night, I assumed Dad would not be at the service. I didn’t realize the Magnolia church would be included.”

“You’re not the one who created that scene,” Ryan pointed out. “He accosted you.”

“He was right,” she admitted bluntly, bowing her head. “I’ve done some things I’m not very proud of, Ryan.”

“We’ve all done things we’re not proud of, Ivy,” he told her gently.

She shook her head as if to say he couldn’t possibly understand. “I just never thought that he would say those things. I mean, I never really thought he’d want anyone else to know about—” She broke off, biting her lip.

Ryan’s heart felt like it weighed about fifty pounds. “You don’t owe me any apologies or explanations, Ivy.”

“That’s kind of you to say,” she mumbled.

“Your sister doesn’t seem to agree with your father,” he noted.

Ivy gave him a smile then, just a small one. "Thankfully. She invited me to Easter dinner, too, but this blasted headache…" She rubbed her forehead. "If you'll excuse me, I—I think I'll just rest." Abruptly, she stepped back and closed the door.

Ryan lifted his hand, but then paused. For several long seconds he stood there, turning away, then back. Part of him couldn't help feeling sorry for Ivy or wanting to comfort her. Another part, even though it left him feeling like a heel, almost wished she hadn't come back to town, that he hadn't sat down at her table last night or issued his ill-fated invitation. He had the feeling that his life had suddenly become much more complicated somehow.

Finally, he faced the fact that the moment to reach out had passed. His steps dragging uncertainly, he took himself back to the apartment and the disappointed faces of his family.

Chapter Five

"Martin and Maria Esquivel are the perfect solution," Charlotte insisted gently.

"Martin does have a background in hotel management," Ty pointed out, glancing around the table. "He's worked at everything from night clerk to concierge."

"And Maria is as hardworking as they come," Charlotte added.

"I don't know," Hap said, grimacing at Charlotte. "I suppose they could have your old room, then if they don't work out—"

"No, Granddad," Charlotte interrupted. "They have an eight-year-old daughter who will need a room of her own. Besides, we can't very well ask them to give up their jobs in Dallas and move here on a trial basis."

Hap sighed and looked down at his hands. The

motel had been his livelihood for nearly half a century, his own personal calling, and Ryan's heart went out to him. So much had changed so fast lately.

For years it had been just the four of them, him, his brother, his sister and their granddad. Now, within the space of mere months, both Charlotte and Holt had married, and while everyone was happy about it, it had taken a toll on Hap's well-ordered existence. No longer able to manage the physical work that came with running the motel, he had relied first on Charlotte and then on Cara for assistance. Holt and Ryan had pitched in for a little while before Cara had come along—okay, mostly Holt—and they had discovered then how difficult, if not impossible, hiring good help had become, given the area's small labor pool and the demands of the booming oil and gas industry on it.

Had Cara not been running from her overbearing in-laws and desperate for work, the motel would likely be sitting on the auction block now. Holt could not have continued neglecting his drilling business for much longer, and the demands of Ryan's profession had certainly not abated, nor would they until the summer and then only for a short time.

"Still time to pray on it," Holt noted, but Ryan saw the glance he flashed at Cara and the secretive smile that tilted her lips.

Wouldn't be long now, Ryan told himself, before

the family would be celebrating the announcement of yet another new addition to the family. To his surprise, the idea settled with as much dismay as satisfaction, which made no sense whatsoever. Hap's life would be turned upside down if Cara could no longer help out with the motel, but all that would really mean for Ryan would be another nephew or niece to love. No reason why he should feel so blue all of a sudden.

He glanced at Ace, and the little boy's gaze zipped up from the minced ham he was intent on cramming into his mouth. Ace could lock in on the least scrap of attention like a homing pigeon sighting its coop, and he beamed his new uncle a toothy smile, all four components of which were recent acquisitions. Some unfamiliar string twanged inside Ryan's chest. Mentally gulping, he gave the little guy a wink before dropping his attention to his plate.

As usual, the ladies had put together a fine meal, combining Charlotte's down-home expertise with Cara's California sensibility. Ham with red-eye gravy, fluffy mashed potatoes and greens spiced with onion and bacon combined with steamed broccoli and almonds, bell peppers stuffed with chopped zucchini and pineapple, whole wheat dinner rolls and thick tomato slices broiled with cheese. Even Charlotte's exquisite deviled eggs had been paired with slices of creamy California avocado, to excellent, if eclectic, effect.

Ryan concentrated on eating as much of the bounty as he could manage. His own bachelor household rarely contained more than dry cereal, canned soup and minimal sandwich makings. Those few items and a bag of potato chips pretty much comprised his weekly shopping list as he ate most of his lunches at the school cafeteria and dinner at this very table as many times a week as he could manage, which wasn't as often as he'd have liked given the many after-school activities that required his presence.

Intent on his food, he missed the conversational switch, only belatedly becoming aware that it now somehow centered on him.

"What?" he asked, looking around in confusion.

His sister glared down at him from the far side of the table, a heavily laden plate in her hands. "Are you going to take this out to Ivy or not?"

Momentarily dumbfounded, he glanced from Hap's calm visage to Holt's challenging one and then on to Ty's muted expression of apologetic sympathy. A picture of Ivy's tearstained face materialized before his mind's eye, and a tumult of contradictory emotions exploded inside his chest. Compassion, dread, excitement, apprehension, curiosity and suspicion all combined into a toxic brew, overlaid by a sudden, unfamiliar surge of irritation.

He simply couldn't figure out why his family expected him to interact with Ivy again. Didn't they have the least understanding of his situation here? Despite that, hadn't he done as they'd asked before and invited Ivy to join them for dinner? He had even urged her, with honest concern, to accept the invitation. What more did they want from him? He looked at his sister and brother-in-law, then his brother and sister-in-law, and it dawned on him.

Matchmaking. They were trying to pair him up with Ivy Villard!

Disgusted, he shoved his chair back from the table and did something so rare that he shocked even himself: He let his temper ignite.

"No!" he barked. "And I don't appreciate all this pressure!"

Four gaping mouths and one sagely speculative look were the last things he saw before he snagged his coat from the back of his chair and slammed out of the room. The latter remained with him the longest. The light of conjecture in his grandfather's eyes disturbed him even more than his own uncharacteristic outburst, for it seemed to contain a knowledge that Ryan feared he might have missed, knowledge about himself.

He tried to tell himself that his family did not seem to consider his responsibility to the community at all. Did the marriages of his siblings suddenly give them greater standing within the family hierarchy than him? Didn't his calling weigh as heavily with them as Ty's position as

CEO of Aldrich and Associates and Holt's business as a wildcatter and oil driller?

That tactic worked for a while, almost until he turned his late-model, midsize domestic sedan into the narrow drive of his house on the northeast side of town. More than half a century old, with pristine white siding and a modern, white composition shingle roof, the house stood flanked on three sides by deep, welcoming porches, hemmed in on either end by sturdy chimneys of dark red brick.

He'd fallen in love with the place at first sight. Being all of ten years old at the time, it hadn't occurred to him that he might own it one day. Over the years, he'd made time to travel past the place whenever he could, just to gaze at its homey, welcoming exterior and note the little changes, some good, some not so much, that time and its owners inflicted. At one point, it had seemed almost derelict, with peeling paint, broken windows and sagging porches. Then, a couple from a neighboring community had bought the place and brought it back to life, renovating and updating. When her mother died, the couple had chosen to move their family into her ailing father's house in order to care for him, and that's how the house on Magnolia Avenue had come into Ryan's hands.

"Solid as a rock," the previous owner had told him, "and more interesting than a new house. No, sir, they don't build them like this anymore."

The house, as he well knew, had been intended for a family, and it had, indeed, nurtured several. He hoped that it would again one day, after him, but for the first time that thought came with a pang that he simply did not understand, a twinge of dissatisfaction that seemed to match, all too well, that worrisome gleam in his grandfather's eye.

Sitting behind the tinted windows of her hybrid, Ivy gripped the steering wheel and swallowed air in an effort to calm her roiling stomach. Suddenly glad that she hadn't been able to do better justice to the plate of food that Ryan's sweet sister-in-law, Cara, had brought over to her room last night, Ivy pressed a hand to her abdomen and whispered a prayer for strength and courage.

She had spent much of Easter evening confessing the selfishness and envy that fed her dread of this meeting, yet here she sat, trembling with the need to run right back to her room and lock the door. Logically, she knew that option held no solution for her. She had been over this a million times in her mind and could find only one way forward. Her father might spurn her apologies and publicly vilify her name, but her sister offered a measure of forgiveness and acceptance that Ivy simply could not ignore. After all she had done, to refuse her sister's outstretched hand would be unforgivable.

Oh, but why, she asked herself, hadn't she considered the possibility that Rose might have children by now? Then again, Ivy already knew the answer to that question. She hadn't considered that possibility because she hadn't been able to face it. Her heartbreak and guilt had prevented her from thinking about children, especially children her good and wholesome sister might have.

Rose was the good daughter who had abandoned neither her principles nor her father. She had married a man he approved of, and she undoubtedly mothered her children with love and pride. For that she deserved the esteem of her family and friends. Even Ivy admired her for the course she had taken and the life she had built. Yes, Rose deserved every good blessing, and if Ivy could not be the wife and mother that Rose was, at least from now on she could be the sister that Rose deserved, even if that meant being an aunt to Rose's children.

Knowing that if she gave herself one more moment to consider she would flee like the coward she was, Ivy opened the car door and slipped out to dash across the street to the simple two-story home. Sitting as it did on Hydrangea Lane in one of the newer neighborhoods on the south side of Eden, the lot lacked the overarching majesty of the ancient trees that graced so much of the small town. It made up for that lack, however, with an abundance of mature evergreen hedges, thick grass and neat, gracefully flowing flowerbeds, which currently boasted a very colorful, if somewhat regimented, display of yellow and red tulips. Although clearly too narrow for it, the flat stoop boasted a green metal glider to one side of the glass-fronted storm door and a large, terra-cotta flower pot overflowing with pink silk hydrangea blossoms, a tribute, no doubt, to the name of the street.

Ivy had barely removed her finger from the doorbell button when her sister appeared in the dark entry hall, a smile of welcome on her face despite her swollen ankles and ungainly girth. She seemed to have gotten even bigger in the past day and a half, her maternity T-shirt stretched taut across her belly. With her brown hair pulled back into a ponytail and her face devoid of cosmetics, she looked far too young to be so pregnant.

Rose pushed open the door and wrapped Ivy in a milk-and-cereal-scented hug, whispering, "I was afraid you wouldn't come."

"So was I," Ivy admitted with a watery chortle.

Rose turned and, waddling, led Ivy down the long, narrow hallway to the large family room at the center of the house. Two little boys with the raven black hair, brown eyes and square face of their father looked up from the carpeted floor, where they sat watching the television in the corner. Rose picked up a remote control device from the dark blue plush sofa and aimed it at the

TV, shutting off the set. The oldest of the boys got to his feet. Wearing gray knit sweats and white socks, his dark hair sticking up in the back due to a cowlick at the crown of his head, he looked positively adorable, if a little solemn.

His mother dropped a hand on his shoulder, saying, "This is Hunter. He's just about to turn five."

That would make him a full year younger than Chelsea, Ivy thought as Rose completed the introduction, identifying her as their aunt.

"Hello," she said, hating the tentative sound of her voice.

A smile broke across Hunter's face. Full of joyous welcome and instant acceptance, that smile warmed Ivy in places she had not even realized were frozen until they began to thaw. Little Scott, not quite three, flopped back onto his elbows and eyed Ivy with wary curiosity. Dressed in jeans, a bright red shirt sporting more than one stain, and faded red socks, he seemed slighter and more like his mom than his big brother.

"Takes him a minute to warm up," Rose said without the least censure or concern in her voice. "Sit down while I get us something to drink."

"Don't put yourself out," Ivy insisted.

Rose blithely ignored her, turning toward the kitchen. "Coffee or tea?"

"Coffee, if you have it."

"Decaf or regular?" Rose asked.

"Premium," Ivy quipped, folding herself down onto the edge of the comfortable sofa. "I need all the caffeine I can get."

Laughing, Rose began opening and closing doors in the kitchen while Ivy sat and smiled stiltedly at her nephews. Scott flopped back and forth on the floor, silently flirting with her, while Hunter picked up a chunky yellow toy truck and brought it to her for examination.

"Very nice."

"It goes by itself," he announced, "when it's got batteries."

"I see."

Unable to resist, she smoothed a hand over his side beneath his arm, feeling the sturdiness of his ribs. Suddenly, she found herself engulfed in an exuberant hug. It was all she could do not to weep. Then, obviously determined not to be left out, Scott launched himself at her, and she was lost. Hopelessly enchanted, heartbreakingly in love, she laughed and cried and covered the tears with more laughter and, eventually, cups of hot, black coffee and her sister's calm, easy conversation.

Gradually, the awkwardness fell away and gladness settled in. For the first time, Ivy tasted a subtle hint of redemption and found it sweet, indeed. She silently thanked God for giving her the courage not to miss out on one of the happiest mornings of her life.

* * *

Shielding his eyes against the setting sun that currently painted the metal bleachers across the field in blinding brilliance, Ryan struggled to make out the form that materialized from the glare. To his surprise, he recognized Daniel Halsey, Ivy's brother-in-law. Something told Ryan that Dan's appearance in the sports stadium on this Monday afternoon had nothing to do with his coaching responsibilities. The middle school track team often worked out in the stadium, of course, but Daniel primarily coached baseball. Then again, Ryan primarily coached football, but here he was, helping to supervise the boys' varsity track team at their after-school practice.

He waited until it became obvious that Daniel had come specifically to see him before he gave the head track coach a nod and moved off to intercept Dan on the turf in the center of the football field.

They greeted each other with handshakes and nods before Dan asked, "Got a minute?"

"Sure. What's up?"

Daniel slid his hands into the pockets of his pleated khakis and ducked his head. Ryan told himself that this unexpected visit could have to do with any number of subjects—from the condition of the rubber track that encircled the football field to a behavior issue with some older student—but he knew instinctively that Dan had come about Ivy. Ryan pursed his lips and waited.

"Has Ivy told you when she's leaving?"

Surprised on several levels by the question, if not the subject, Ryan shook his head. "Why would you be asking me that? You're her brother-in-law. Surely you have more reason to know Ivy's plans than I would."

Daniel sighed and said, "We had no clue that she was even coming to town, and since Rose mentioned that you took her to the sunrise service yesterday, I thought maybe Ivy had discussed her plans with you."

"I didn't exactly take her to the service," Ryan hedged uncomfortably. "We walked over together from the motel, that's all." He waited a heartbeat before adding, "I guess you know what went on there with Olie."

Daniel made a face. "I know he said some unkind things."

"Unkind?" Ryan scoffed. "They were more than that, Dan. The whole thing was downright ugly. I had no idea that Olie could be so nasty, especially to his own daughter."

Anger flashed across Daniel's usually placid face. "You don't have to tell me about either one of them. Those two have been putting my wife through an emotional wringer for years, and frankly, I'm tired of it."

Ryan frowned thoughtfully before saying, "Look, I don't know anything about your family business, but what happened yesterday is all on Olie. His hateful words crushed Ivy, reduced her to tears. She tried to be civil, but he wouldn't have it."

Daniel winced. "It's just the timing of this whole thing. This pregnancy has been difficult for Rose, and she doesn't need a lot of emotional upset right now."

"I'm sorry to hear that," Ryan said, clapping a hand down on Dan's shoulder. "I'll be sure to pray for her."

"Thank you," Daniel smiled wanly. "I appreciate that, but I can't help worrying. Of all the times that Ivy could have picked to visit, this is the worst."

"I'm sure Ivy wants only the best for her sister."

"Who knows what Ivy wants?" Daniel grumbled.

"Maybe you should just explain the situation to her," Ryan counseled. "She'll understand and do her part to spare Rose any unnecessary upset."

"You think? Because if Ivy gets upset with me, then Rose will, too. In fact, if Rose even gets wind of such a conversation, she'll be fit to be tied. I know it."

Before Ryan could formulate a reply to that, the satellite phone in his hip pocket vibrated and began playing the Eden Memorial High School fight song. Right after Tyler had given the family these nifty little phones, owing to the problematic cell service in the area, Ryan had searched the Internet for the tune and downloaded it himself, much to the amusement of his students, coworkers, family and friends. Shrugging apologetically, Ryan snatched the phone and glanced at the screen. He frowned at his companion.

"Dan, that's you calling."

"Me? Must be Rosie calling from the house, but why would she call you?"

Ryan held up a stalling hand, pressed the green button and lifted the tiny phone to his ear. "Ryan Jefford here."

"Ryan," Ivy's voice gasped. "You've got to help me. Rose won't let me call the police, but I can't find Daniel, and I don't dare leave her alone here with the boys!"

Alarm flashed through him, but also a leveling calm. "It's all right. Dan's here with me."

"Oh, thank God! Thank God! I just couldn't think who else to call!"

He assumed that Ivy had gotten his cell number either by calling his office and listening to the message he had recorded or by calling the motel, but he really couldn't have cared less at the moment. "Is Rose okay?" he asked, switching his gaze to Daniel's already fearful face.

"No. She's in labor, and it's too early."

"Have you called an ambulance?"

"It'll take at least a half-hour for them to get here. I don't think she can wait."

Ryan saw the panic dawning in Daniel's dark eyes and knew that the other man would be out of his mind with worry as soon as he heard this news. Ryan could think of only one thing to do: He'd have to drive Daniel home, and then they'd see.

"We're on our way," he told Ivy, ending the call.

While Daniel constantly skimmed his hand through his hair in agitation, Ryan quickly guided the sedan through the streets of Eden. In an effort to calm the other man, Ryan began to pray aloud, speaking the thoughts that had been circling through his mind since Ivy had called.

"Lord, Your timing is perfect and always works to our best, but we're frightened about the possibility of Rose's baby coming too early. Please protect Rose and her child. Prepare the way and help us be calm and careful. Comfort Rose, Daniel, Ivy and the boys. Give the doctors wisdom and skill, and cradle that precious new life and tiny body in Your protective hands. Protect Rose and her health and return her quickly to her home and the loving arms of her husband and sons."

He kept on in that vein until they pulled into the driveway of the Halsey house, where a horrific sight met them. Rose leaned on Ivy's supportive arm as she hobbled toward her minivan, her olive knit slacks stained. Ivy clutched a stack of towels even as she rushed Rose toward the drive, the boys on her heels.

Daniel bailed out of the car even before it came

to a complete stop, screaming, "What happened? What happened?"

"I think her water just broke!" Ivy exclaimed.

Rose reached for her husband as he ran toward her, saying calmly, "I called Dr. Harpetra. He'll meet us in Duncan." She gasped and grabbed her belly with both hands.

"Can you hold on that long?" Daniel asked in an agonized voice.

"No choice," she managed as Ryan arrived. Ivy stepped aside, and Daniel slid into place, wrapping both arms around Rose to help support her weight.

Together Daniel and Ryan helped Rose take a few more steps to the van and handed her through the open sliding door. Ivy passed the towels to Daniel, and he climbed in next to Rose. Ryan and Ivy looked at each other.

"Someone has to stay with the boys," she said, an arm around each of the two raven-haired kids, both with wide, fearful eyes.

Ryan glanced at his car and then the van before digging into his pocket for his keys. "Move my car out of the way, will you?"

"You'll call as soon as you can?"

"Absolutely."

Ivy sent the boys to the house and poked her head into the van. Ryan hurried around to the driver's seat, hearing her say, "Rose, I love you.

Don't worry about anything here." With that, she ran for the sedan.

Ryan slid behind the steering wheel, snatching the keys that dangled from Daniel's trembling hand. Taking a deep breath, he backed the vehicle down the drive and aimed it toward the two-lane highway that would take them the thirty-five or so miles north to the hospital in Duncan.

Once they reached Highway 81, Ryan took out his phone and hit the autodial to call his grandfather and spread the news.

"I'll call out the troops," Hap said. "You tell Rose we're praying for her and the baby. I'll get in touch with her pastor, too, so their church will know."

Ryan passed that information along, and Daniel immediately seized on it. "That's good. That's good. Isn't that good, honey?"

Rose grit out, "Yes," and after several moments of rough panting said, "Good for Ivy to stay with the boys, too."

"Let's don't worry about Ivy right now!" Daniel snapped.

Ryan felt compelled to point out that having Ivy there to stay with the boys was a blessing.

"For her, too," Rose muttered, but then she moaned and began to sob.

Ryan didn't know beans about having babies, but this scenario struck him as all wrong, from Rose's size to the blood he'd seen and her continuous state of pain. A chill swept over him. Feeling considerably more urgency than before, he picked up his prayer again, a steady stream of words falling out of his mouth with more eloquence than they formed inside his head.

"Father God, Creator of life, Keeper of souls, help us in this our hour of need..." he said and pressed the accelerator, hard.

Chapter Six

"Rose is stable," the diminutive doctor said in his lilting foreign accent. "No pain at all for present, just discomfort now."

Daniel closed his eyes. "Thank God. I've never seen her like that before. Her labor with the boys was different."

"No labor," the doctor said. "This was not labor."

"So the baby's not coming, yet?" Daniel asked, sounding confused. "I thought once her water broke that the baby had to come."

Dr. Harpetra bobbed his head and continued in his melodic voice, "Her water, it did not break. The bleeding from secondary source." He went on to explain, in more detail than Ryan frankly wanted to hear, what had happened, finishing with, "This is now under control."

Olie rushed into the small private parlor where

they had waited to hear the doctor's report. Daniel had called him from Ryan's phone as soon as Rose had started receiving treatment in the Emergency Room. "How is she?" Olie demanded breathlessly. Everyone turned his way, and brief introductions were made.

"Your daughter is stable," the doctor explained, "but she has lost much blood." He turned his intelligent gaze on Daniel again and gently added, "The concern now is for baby."

"What do you mean?"

"This has been difficult pregnancy from beginning, as we know," the slight physician said. "High pressure with excess fluid can compress placenta, which maybe does not properly feed child as she develop in utero." He patted Daniel on the upper arm, adding, "Now Mama rest. Then we test for viability of infant."

"Viability," Daniel whispered. "You're telling me that we could lose the baby?"

The doctor merely gave the worried father a consoling smile. "We will talk more later." With that, he left the room.

For a moment, all three men stood in stunned silence. Then Olie shifted his feet. Looking a little lost and uncertain, he asked in a thick voice, "Where're the boys?"

Daniel shook his head as if still trying to make sense of what the doctor had told them, so Ryan provided the answer, thoughtlessly muttering, "At home with Ivy."

Olie erupted, throwing up his arms and yelling, "Ivy! At home with *Ivy?*" He grabbed Daniel by the arm, demanding, "Are you out of your mind? You know what she is! You know that—"

"Shut up!" Daniel yelled, turning on him. "I don't want to hear it! I'm sick of hearing it. Rose is sick of...Rose is sick," he finished in an agonized voice.

Olie's eyes sparkled with tears, but he turned down his mouth and huffed, "I blame *her* for this. She never should've come back. Disaster follows wherever Ivy goes."

Ryan could not believe his ears. "That's an outrageous thing to say. You heard the doctor. This has been a difficult pregnancy from the start. You can't blame Ivy for that. Ivy was there today when Rose and Dan needed her," Ryan pointed out harshly. It incensed him that Olie couldn't give her that much credit, at least.

"And maybe they wouldn't have needed her if she hadn't been there!" Olie cried. "She obviously upset Rosie!"

"You don't know that Ivy upset Rose!"

"I know that if Rose hadn't been dealing with her no-good sister, maybe she'd be home right now with her feet up like she's supposed to be!"

"You just want to blame Ivy," Ryan accused.

"She's got you fooled, I see," Olie sneered. "But

I know her." He thumped himself in the chest. "Just like I knew her man-crazy mama!"

"Enough!" Daniel snapped at his father-in-law. "Either shut up or go, Olie. I don't have the patience for one of your rants."

Olie steamed, glaring at Ryan, but in the end, he turned and walked over to a chair, dropping down between its lightly padded arms. Ryan glowered, more than a little irritated with both of them, himself and Olie. It had been a long time since his temper had ignited so easily, and now twice in as many days he'd lost it. He knew that Olie was upset about Rose and the baby. They all were. Still, Olie could not have chosen a less appropriate time to vent his spleen. Olie seemed to have a problem with that, at least so far as it pertained to Ivy. Whatever she had done, it couldn't have merited such venom.

Daniel eased up to Ryan. "I hate to impose on you anymore. You've already done so much."

"No, no. I'll help any way I can." Ryan hung his head, feeling guilt. "And I apologize for my part in the argument, but his attitude toward Ivy borders on irrational."

Nodding, Daniel leaned closer still and whispered, "That's why I need you to check on Ivy and the boys." Ryan felt the familiar mix of dread and excitement. Dan passed a hand over his forehead, saying, "They must be so scared."

Ryan softened. Of course, Daniel would be concerned for his sons. What father would not be? Ryan had to return to the house for his car anyway. Besides, he had promised to call Ivy with news, and news like this ought to be delivered in person. "Okay. But will you be all right here?" He glanced at Olie.

"Yeah, yeah. He's got it out of his system for the time being." Daniel scrubbed a hand over his face and said, "I'm not going anywhere until I know everything's all right, and my folks are on their way here, so will you ask Ivy to stay with the boys tonight or at least until I can arrange something else?"

"Don't worry about that," Ryan told him. "If for some reason Ivy can't stay the night, my family will be glad to take care of the boys. I'll stay myself if necessary, though my experience is with older kids, as you might imagine."

Daniel looked relieved. "I appreciate that, Ryan. As for the van, just leave it at the house for now. We'll figure out how to get it back up here later."

Davis Latimer, the young pastor of the Magnolia church, arrived just then and walked straight to Daniel with his arms outstretched. The two men embraced. Then, with tears standing in his eyes, Daniel thanked him for coming.

"How are they?"

Before Dan could begin an explanation of the situation, Ryan took his leave. "Call if you need anything else."

Daniel gripped his hand. “Thank you. Thank you for everything.”

“I’ll keep in touch. Try not to worry. Lots of prayers are going up.”

The pastor seconded that, and Ryan left the two men talking softly. As soon as he got out of the building, he phoned Ivy at Rose’s house, telling her only that Rose was stable and in no pain.

“I’ll fill you in on the details when I get there,” he promised, noting that he had left Daniel in the company of his pastor and her father.

Ivy sucked in a deep breath and said only, “I’ll be waiting.”

Ryan walked out to Rose Halsey’s minivan with a heavy heart and mixed emotions. So much for not getting sucked in. Part of him thanked God that he’d been with Daniel when Ivy had called, the other part wished he had been anywhere else.

Sitting forward on the couch, Ivy stopped herself before she could push up to her feet. Pacing would do no good, and the boys were already on edge, wondering when Mom and Dad would be home. Hunter had enough understanding of the situation to inform his little brother that their parents would be returning with a baby, but Scott hotly denied any such thing.

“Uh-uh. We gettin’ a sister.”

“That don’t mean we’re not getting a baby, goof.”

"Babies is boys."

That momentarily stymied Hunter, as he clearly remembered the advent of a baby brother into his personal realm. "Well, you were an ugly one," he declared, "and stinky, too."

The resulting fight consisted of two poorly aimed blows and a lot of wailing. Afterward, at Ivy's suggestion, they apologized to each other, a skill at which both seemed to have lots of experience. Then the two of them crawled up into Ivy's lap for "a read," as Hunter put it. It was nice, Scott allowed, that she had room for both of them.

"We have to sit *beside* Mom," Hunter pointed out.

"But we can sit in her lap when the sister comes," Scott remarked, offering Ivy a choice of his favorite books by smacking her in the chin with them.

Later, with much advice from Hunter, Ivy cobbled together a simple dinner of fish sticks, green beans and shoestring potatoes liberally adorned with ketchup, which taught her never to allow little boys to serve their own condiments. Bellies full and mess cleaned up, they sprawled on the family room floor scribbling in coloring books while Ivy tried to find some way, with the dishes done, to occupy her thoughts.

She dared not think of the child Rose might even now be having or the darker worry that hovered in the back of her mind. Having had some familiarity with childbirth, Ivy knew that what Rose had experienced that afternoon when she'd suddenly doubled over in screaming pain was not the norm, but she had tried mightily not to dwell on that.

The sound of the doorbell gave her a reason to get up and fix her attention elsewhere. Swiftly, she walked down the long, narrow hallway to the front of the house. Ryan stood on the other side of the glass storm door, still wearing the same green jogging suit with "Coach" emblazoned on it in yellow letters outlined in white. Full night had descended, and she switched on the lights, inside and out, while releasing the latch.

"How was she when you left?"

"Just as I told you on the phone, stable and in no pain."

"They're expecting a short labor then? They've already given her the spinal block?"

Ryan rubbed his jaw, rough with the golden glint of day-old stubble. "I'm, um, not very good with the vernacular of childbirth. Why don't we sit down? I'll tell you what I think I heard the doctor saying."

Nodding, she led him into the center of the house. The boys sat cross-legged, facing the doorway expectantly. Ryan smiled at them, then glanced a warning at Ivy. A chill of foreboding swept over her, the same chill that she had been holding at bay all evening. Turning to the boys, she put on her lightest expression.

"Hunter, would you like to take your brother

into the kitchen for a snack? I left half a dozen cookies on the table."

She'd meant them for a bedtime enticement, expecting that she would be here at least long enough to bribe them into crawling between the sheets. The boys scrambled up and flew into the kitchen amid cries of, "Me first!" Ivy smiled at their greedy delight before inviting Ryan to take a seat next to her on the blue sofa. She had the feeling, one with which she was all too familiar, that she ought to smile while she could.

"Something's wrong," she surmised softly.

As if to confirm her suspicions, Ryan grasped her hand in his. "There was some kind of bleeding, not the normal kind, but the doctors stopped that. I don't understand it all, and I don't think I want to, but from what I gleaned, Rose will be okay."

"Rose," Ivy repeated warily. "Please tell me she hasn't lost the baby."

Ryan's big, warm hand squeezed hers. "No, but it doesn't sound good. As soon as she's rested, they're going to do some tests to check on the baby. The term 'viability' was used."

Ivy squeezed her eyes shut and bit her lip. Her poor sister. To lose a child was the worst of pains, especially when everyone expected and wanted, looked forward to, a healthy baby. She shook her head, refusing to give in to pessimism and fear.

"It could still turn out all right. It's early for the

baby but not terribly so. God is in control here. We have to hold on to that."

"Yes. That's right," Ryan said with a smile. "The tests could all show a healthy baby."

"When will they know?"

He shook his head. "No one said, but Dan asked if you could stay the night."

She nodded vigorously. "Of course. No problem. Except… all my things are at the motel."

From the kitchen came the sound of a screeching chair and then the bellow, "Give it back!"

Ivy lifted her eyebrows and rose to her feet, saying, "Excuse me a moment."

With Ryan following, she hurried to the kitchen, where she found Scott standing on a chair and holding a cookie as high over his head as he could manage while Hunter fumed with folded arms.

"That's *my* cookie! He gobbles his, and then he takes mine!"

Scott didn't wait to be instructed to return the cookie in question, just tossed it and plopped down. Hunter made a good catch and began nibbling on the prize, taking the smallest bites imaginable. A thoroughly unrepentant Scott looked at Ivy and demanded, "Milk, please."

She heard a muffled chuckle behind her as she went to the cabinet for a glass.

"Who're you?" Hunter asked.

"Mr. Jefford," Ryan said. "I work with your dad."

"Oh. That's why you got the same clothes, I guess."

"That's right."

"Orange cup!" Scott yelled at Ivy.

"Blue," Hunter corrected, adding, "He wets the bed if he gets the orange cup 'cause it's too much."

"I don't wet the bed!" Scott refuted, scrambling once more to his feet. "I got pull-ups. See?" With that he dropped his jeans, shoved them right down to his ankles, demanding, "Orange cup!"

"Blue," Ivy said firmly, turning for the refrigerator. She took out the milk and carried cup and carton to the table, where Scott still stood on his chair with his pants around his ankles. He gave Ryan a look that seemed to ask what he was waiting for. After a moment, Ryan ambled over and yanked up the jeans.

"I think you'd better learn not to stand on chairs," Ryan said, hiding a smile behind a stern expression, "because you can fall and hurt yourself."

"Okay." Squatting, Scott stretched out his legs. Planted once more on his bottom, he reached for his cup.

Ivy saw the amusement in Ryan's green-and-gold eyes. "You go get your things," he told her. "I'll stay here until you get back."

She looked at the boys, then smiled at Ryan. "Thanks. I won't be long."

Hurrying from the room, she heard Hunter say, "I want milk, too. Orange cup."

"Yes on the milk," Ryan said. "No on the orange cup. If your brother can't have it, neither can you."

Not a single word of argument followed, just the sound of heavy footsteps crossing the kitchen floor and a little boy giggling into his milk.

"Your mom's in the hospital," Ryan explained, "so the doctors can take care of her, and your dad's there so she won't be scared."

"Is she coming home?" Hunter asked, the huskiness of his tone revealing his concern.

"Sure." Sitting between them on the couch, Ryan gave the older boy's head a rub. "Could be a few days, though. But don't worry. Your Aunt Ivy is coming back to spend the night."

"Who is Aunt Ivy?" Hunter asked.

Confused, Ryan gave him the first answer that came into his head. "The lady who was here earlier."

"No, I mean, who *is* she? Aunt Lolly is Daddy's sister, and Aunt Moon is Grandpa Halsey's sister, but whose sister is Aunt Ivy?"

"Ivy is your mother's sister," Ryan explained.

"No, she's not." Both boys shook their heads. "Grandpa Olie said so."

"You must have misunderstood," Ryan said, taking a firm grip on his temper. "I've known your mother and your Aunt Ivy my whole life, and they are sisters."

Scott leaned into him, his sharp little elbow

digging into Ryan's thigh. "How come we never knowed her before?" he asked.

"You've never met your Aunt Ivy before?"

"Nope."

"Never," Hunter confirmed. "On account of she's a tramp." He screwed up his face. "What is a tramp?"

Rocked, Ryan could only demand, "Where did you hear such an ugly word?"

"Grandpa said it," Scott tattled, "when him and Mama shouted one time."

"No one should use that word," Ryan counseled, mentally gritting his teeth, "not even your grandfather, and I want you both to promise that you won't say it again, especially not in front of your Aunt Ivy."

Hunter promised. Scott sat up, relieving the pressure on Ryan's thigh, and confessed, "That's what Mama told us." He went on, obviously repeating words he had tried to memorize. "Don't talk what Grandpa Olie says front of Ivy."

"Your mother is right," Ryan said.

"Grandpa don't like Aunt Ivy," Hunter said, "but Mom does, and I do, too."

"Me, too," Scott chimed in. "She gives us cookies and her lap's got no belly there."

Ryan had to bite his lip to keep from laughing. "Well, that makes all of us then," he said, "because I like Ivy, too. Now, what'll we do until she gets back?"

"Wrestle!" Scott yelled, popping up onto his knees and launching himself at Ryan's head.

* * *

Ivy didn't stop to figure out what to take, just tossed everything back into the bag and zipped it closed. The idea of dropping in to tell Hap Jefford what was going on crossed Ivy's mind, but she really wanted to get back to the boys and relieve Ryan as quickly as possible. Besides, she reasoned, Ryan would tell his family about Rose's situation soon, if he hadn't already. She would mention it to him when she got back to the house. The more people who were praying for Rose and the baby, the better, to Ivy's way of thinking.

She'd been sending up quick, desperate prayers from the moment Rose had first doubled over in pain, so she took her time to do a little better job of it on her way back across town.

Dear Lord, please take care of my sister and her baby. Losing a child is the worst thing, but You would know that, wouldn't You? That's what I tell myself when I think about Chelsea. You gave up Your Son to the cross, willingly allowing His sacrifice to pay the sin debt for all the rest of us. I gave up my daughter for her own sake. I was too stupid and selfish to be the mommy she needed. But Rose hasn't done the kind of things I have, Lord. She's a good mother. She doesn't deserve to lose her baby. Please, please take care of them, for Rose and Daniel and everyone who loves them. And thank You for not letting me chicken out today. I'm so glad I was there when Rose needed me, and thank You for Ryan being with Dan, too. I know, I know, You'll take care of my sister and her baby. In the name of Jesus, amen.

She parked her car behind Rose's minivan in front of the single-bay garage, grabbed her bag and hurried around to the front door. Laughter greeted her, the mindless, joyous, giggling mirth of two small children at play.

Correction, she told herself a moment later, smiling as she stood in the doorway of the family room. *Make that two small children and one overgrown boy.*

All three rolled across the floor in a tangle of arms and legs. Ryan landed flat on his back with the boys sprawled across his green-clad legs and broad, yellow-shirted chest. He had removed his jacket and left it draped over the back of the overstuffed chair that matched the sofa. His boat-sized white athletic shoes stood neatly against the wall beside the doorway. Suddenly he jackknifed, catching both boys in his arms, and flipped, pinning them to the floor with his weight levered onto his forearms and knees.

"Now I gotcha!"

They howled in protest, laughing and squirming with delight. "No fair! No fair! You're bigger than us!"

"Hey, two against one," Ryan pointed out, folding

himself into a sitting position. He scooted until his back came up against the foot of the sofa. Panting slightly, he raked his hands through his wavy hair in an effort to smooth it. Scott got up and threw himself at Ryan, screaming like a banshee, but Ryan easily caught the boy and sat him in his lap. "Match over. Your aunt's home."

Hunter dragged himself over to lean against Ryan's shoulder. "Hoo, boy, that was a good one," he said. "Dad could get some lessons from you."

Ryan ruffled the boy's thick hair. "He's taught you some pretty good moves."

"I'm gonna be a coach, too, when I grow up!" Hunter proclaimed.

"Best job in the world," Ryan said, putting back his head to smile up at Ivy. At the same time, Scott curled up and stuck his thumb in his mouth, clearly exhausted.

She felt her heart turn over, and it hit her suddenly how very much she had missed with her unconventional life. She might have had a marriage, a family. She might have had it all, everything that Rose and Daniel had, everything that Brand had proclaimed banal and senseless.

He actually believed that "the breeders," as he called parents, were damaging the planet by overpopulating. He claimed to champion a "new" lifestyle, a "free" lifestyle, the "true" existence that nature had designed, where self-interest meant survival and "selfish" was just a label assigned by a public twisted and browbeaten by religion.

"Live now," he had preached, "for today, this moment."

He had really meant, *Take what you need, do what you want, and don't let anyone make you feel guilty about it.*

Ivy looked at Rose's life and suddenly knew the full value of what she had given up, of what she had traded for "excitement" and ratings. Perhaps she had never really bought into the FireBrand Phillips philosophy, but she had told herself that she wouldn't have been a good mother, anyway, that she didn't truly need what Rose and countless other women had.

Now she knew.

She had given up marriage and family for lies, not for the lies Brand had told her but for the lies she had told herself. As she glanced at Ryan, she felt a sharp pain deep in her heart.

Chapter Seven

The clock over the door had never sounded so loud to Ryan, but he ignored the constant expiration of seconds as well as he could. A little ticking should not bother a lifelong resident of Eden, Oklahoma, where pumps constantly sucked oil, the blood of the local economy, out of the ground. Why, they had a pump jack at work in the parking lot of City Hall, for pity's sake. It had been said that babies elsewhere slept to the comforting beat of their mothers' hearts, but that here in Eden they slept to the steady thump of the oil well.

The thought of babies led to thoughts of the Halseys, which in turn led to thoughts of Ivy Villard…again.

Ryan turned away from the computer screen where he had been devising questions for a test. Pinching the bridge of his nose, he sighed. He had not slept well last night, troubled with thoughts of Rose, Daniel and their unborn baby, Ivy and the boys, Olie and his hostility. None of it could really be called his concern, and he had more than enough to do already; yet he could forget the troubles of that family and the troubles of one dark-haired, dark-eyed lady in particular.

Had the tests turned out well? Was Ivy coping okay with the boys? How could a father hate his own daughter?

The jangling telephone on his desk brought welcome respite from his thoughts. He punched a button and answered without picking up the receiver.

"Mr. Jefford here. How can I help you?"

"Ryan, it's Matt."

Ryan winced but covered his discomfort with a jovial tone. "Hey, Matt, what can I do for you on this Tuesday morning? If it's about the recommendation, I'm afraid I haven't had a chance to actually pray about it yet."

"I understand, but a job's come up that I'm really interested in. It requires two recommendations, and one must come from someone in our field. A single paragraph would take care of it."

"I, um, haven't gotten anything on paper."

"You can do it online. In fact, that's the preferred method. It just has to come from your e-mail address."

Ryan dropped his head into his hand, elbow braced against the top of his desk. "Online, huh?

Guess that's the modern world we live in. Just let me pray about this, Matt, and I'll see what I can put together."

"Listen, I don't mean to pressure you, but there aren't that many opportunities around just now, and this is one I really don't want to miss out on. If you could just go take a look at the Web site, I'd appreciate it."

"Okay, yeah, sure, but wouldn't it be better, um, coming from someone you've actually worked with?"

"No," Matt said flatly. "No, it wouldn't. If you must know, they wouldn't offer, and I wouldn't ask."

"I see," Ryan muttered, not seeing at all. "Would you care to elaborate?"

"Look, Ryan," Matt went on, dropping his voice, "I wouldn't have come to you if I didn't have to. You don't know what we've been through here, and I'll admit that I'm still angry about the whole thing, but I'm trying to get past it. I just need a few lines of recommendation from a respected individual in my field. And they're going to want you to attest to a few statements, but that's it. Nothing you can't do with a clear conscience, I guarantee. Just go the Web site and take a look. Please."

Ryan recognized desperation when he heard it. Even as he jotted down the Web link and promised to take a look, he knew that he would have to pray long and hard before he decided what to do, and he knew, too, that he had to have more information than Matt seemed willing to give him. The way Matt had just spoken discouraged Ryan from asking point-blank why and how Matt had left his last job, but he felt that he had to have that information. Something was just not right.

As soon as he hung up the phone, he bowed his head and folded his hands. He needed guidance—and information. After a brief prayer, he asked the secretary in the outer office to get him the number of a coach he knew who worked at Matt's former school.

Class schedules intervened, so it was late in the day when Ryan and the other coach finally connected. Both had after-school practices to oversee, so Ryan did not mince words. He asked for a full accounting of why and how Matt Barston's employment had been brought to an end at Hilltop.

"Off the record?" the other man asked.

"If necessary."

Ryan had expected some reluctance if not outright refusal. School districts could be touchy about personnel matters, as well they should. He found himself shocked when the fellow eagerly launched into a monologue laced with salacious rumor and innuendo, most of it concerning Matt's wife, Devony. In disbelief, Ryan heard the words *drug addict*, *nude photos* and, most shocking of all, *prostitute*.

"And she admits it," his informant told him, "talks about it in public. Even went on the radio."

Ryan cringed, remembering that he saw Ivy and

Devony together at the reunion. The other fellow rushed on, saying, "You can imagine the talk around here. Quite a few parents went to the school board to complain, but the end came when the photos showed up."

Mentally reeling, Ryan listened to a brief description of explicit pictures posted on the Internet before he interrupted. "So they fired Matt?"

"Technically he resigned, but if you ask me it was just a matter of time before the school board would have been forced to act. They were under a lot of pressure."

Ryan sighed, thanked the fellow and got off the phone. Heartsick, he thought over all he'd been told. If anything, this only made matters worse. Ryan put no stock in gossip, and he certainly would not be checking out any photos of Matt's wife, but if any portion of what he had just heard was true.... To say that he was having great misgivings about writing that recommendation would be a gross understatement.

And what, he had to wonder, did Ivy have to do with Devony's situation?

After a second restless night, Ryan made a point of attending the Wednesday prayer meeting at his church. He tried always to do so but managed to attend only about twice a month. The time had been when no school activity was scheduled in deference to the midweek service, but the pressure of expanded academics and additional student interests had made it difficult to maintain that standard, so on the occasional Wednesday evening Ryan found himself called upon to supervise some school group. On other evenings, especially since Charlotte had married, he manned the motel desk so Hap, Holt and now Cara could attend the prayer group. Tonight, however, he felt the need to be present with others in prayer. Thankfully, Cara and Holt had volunteered to watch the desk.

Ryan found it odd that they both intended to stay behind, but Hap laughed it off saying, "They're in love. Of course they want to be together."

"But they're together so much already," Ryan pointed out. "Guess it's that newlywed thing."

Hap just smiled and shook his head. "The way it worked for your grandma and me," he divulged huskily, "the longer we were together, the more we wanted to be. And the longer she's gone, the more I miss her."

Ryan nodded, silently commenting to himself that not many marriages were so blessed. Happily, those of Charlotte and Holt seemed to be, and certainly Dan and Rose Halsey were devoted to one another, though Ryan couldn't help wondering what the crisis they were going through might mean for their marriage. He had called the hospital earlier, and Daniel's fear had been obvious.

"It's all up to God now," Dan had said. The doctors felt they had to induce labor or risk Rosie's health, but no one could predict whether the baby would make it. Despite Rose's size, the baby had been deemed smaller than she should be. "The boys and I can't lose Rose," Dan had whispered, "but I hate to think what losing the baby would do to her, so I'm just trying to believe that everything will be okay."

Ryan hoped that what they were going through now only strengthened their bond, even as he prayed for the survival and health of both mother and child.

He tried not to think about Ivy or how she might be feeling, but then Olie showed up. It wasn't unusual for members of the Magnolia congregation to show up at the larger midweek prayer service at First Church, given the relationship between the two organizations. Olie came in late, just as the short general service was breaking up into small groups. His long, narrow face looked positively ravaged, and despite the ugliness he'd spewed earlier, Ryan pitied the man—until his prayer request veered from concern for his younger daughter to something else entirely.

"Rosie's a good girl," Olie declared, his voice trembling, "not like...some. I keep wondering if God punishes us for not casting out the immoral from our midst. Isn't that what *Corinthians* tells us to do?"

"I think that passage in *Corinthians* that you're

referring to has to do with gross sexual immorality," the pastor, Grover Waller, pointed out.

"All I'm saying is maybe they got it right over in Hilltop," Olie said. "Barston married up with an immoral woman, and basically they run him out of town."

Several of the men seated in the circle of folding chairs shifted uneasily in their seats.

"Scripture also tells us not to judge and to love others as Jesus loves us, Olie," Hap pointed out gently.

"That's right," Ryan said. "Matt Barston's situation is between him and God."

"Of course, *you* would say that," Olie retorted sourly.

Shaken by the implication, Ryan glanced around the circle of men who had gathered to pray. Most averted their gazes, but whether from discomfort due to Olie's venom or something more personally ominous, Ryan did not know. He gulped, anger simmering just beneath the calm surface that he somehow managed to maintain.

Ryan never mentioned his own concerns. He suddenly didn't know what to ask for. He truly did not want to judge Matt, whom he'd always believed to be a fine Christian man and educator, but he had a certain responsibility to the community and his calling. He felt trapped between that proverbial rock and hard place. For the first time in his adult life, he was confused about what to do. *Right* and *best* no longer seemed to be the same thing.

Instead of the peace and certainty that he had come there seeking, he came away at the end of the evening ashamed without being quite certain why and more baffled than ever. For a third long night, he tossed and turned, his thoughts veering from the Halseys and their unborn child to Matt and Ivy and the individual they seemed to have in common, Matt's wife, Devony.

God in heaven, he prayed, *whatever am I to do?*

The answer came, at least in part, the next afternoon when Ivy called, weeping, to say that Rose had delivered a stillborn daughter.

"Ivy, I'm so sorry," he said. After several moments of unbroken sobbing on the other end of the line, Ryan did something he had never done before. He walked out of his classroom in the middle of a lesson. Some situations just took precedence over everything else.

Within minutes, he stood outside the Halsey house. As usual, the inner door stood open, presumably to let light into the dark, narrow hall, leaving only the glass storm door between him and entry. He reached out a hand to press the doorbell and caught sight of Ivy standing with her back to the wall, silently keening. Just far enough inside to be cloaked by the shadows that seemed to permeate that space, she had covered her face with both hands, but her entire posture, the hunch of her shoulders, the way she had shrunk in on herself, proclaimed a measure of grief that rattled him.

Trying the door, he found that the latch had been released and walked inside. Instinctively, he reached for her. She came into his arms blindly, her slender body racked with strangled sobs. As troubling as he found her sorrow, an unusual calm settled over him. He held her without a word, her face in the hollow of his shoulder, his arms tight about her. Long minutes passed before he felt her gulp and shake her head. Sensing that she had at last asserted some control over her emotions, he turned her and guided her gently down the long passage and into the family room.

Hunter and Scott sat on the floor in front of the TV, close enough to hear with the volume set very low. Neither of them so much as turned a head when Ryan and Ivy entered the room, but Ryan saw that Hunter held the remote and knew that the boy was no doubt responsible for the near silence of the TV. Ryan sat, pulling Ivy down onto the sofa with him. She moved mechanically without the least resistance, one hand fisted in the fabric of his shirt as if to keep him close, but she had yet to look at him.

Tendrils of dark, sleek hair had escaped from a loose ponytail on the back of her head and now wafted haphazardly about her face and shoulders. Giving in to impulse, Ryan reached out to smooth the silky wisps from her cheek, and finally she turned her gaze to his. Her lovely brown eyes, black lashes spiked with tears, contained an agony so sharp that it shredded whatever resistance he might have had. With one hand, he pulled her head down onto his shoulder. Curling into him, she coiled an arm about his neck and thoroughly wet the front of his shirt, her body convulsing in silence.

After what felt like a long while, Hunter got up and came to stand at Ryan's knee. "Aunt Ivy," he said in a soft voice, "can we have cheese crackers for snack?"

Ivy pulled herself together, an incremental process that made Ryan think of bricks going one by one into a wall. Finally, she offered up a wobbly smile and nodded, whispering, "I'll get them." Rising from the couch, she walked toward the kitchen.

Hunter laid a hand on Ryan's knee. Sensing that the boy needed to say something, Ryan watched Ivy for a moment. She seemed steady enough on her feet, so he looked to the boy. Leaning close, Hunter whispered, "No sister."

Ryan pulled the boy up onto his lap. Scott stayed in front of the TV, seemingly hypnotized by the cartoon that played on the screen, but Ryan knew some part of the younger boy was attuned to everything around him.

"I'm sorry about your sister," Ryan said gently.

"For some reason God took her straight to heaven to be with Him, and that's made everyone very sad. We were hoping we could get to know her and watch her grow up. But the good thing is, we already have you guys, and someday, when the time is right, maybe you'll get another little sister."

Hunter nodded. "Aunt Ivy said she was too sick to grow up."

"That's true."

"Mom's sad, too, isn't she?"

"Yes, I'm sure both she and your father are very sad right now, but they must be doubly glad to have you and Scott. I'm sure that they can't wait to come home and see you."

"When will they?"

"As soon as your mom's well enough. Another day or two, I'd think."

"And till then you and Aunt Ivy will take care of us."

You and Aunt Ivy. Ryan's heart knocked hard against the wall of his chest. He suddenly felt paired up. How had that happened? But hadn't he feared, on some level, right from the beginning, that it would? He shook his head before realizing how that would look to Hunter, then quickly reassured the boy.

"That's right. Aunt Ivy and I will take care of you."

Satisfied, Hunter slid off Ryan's lap and went to

sit next to his brother, who said loudly, "I wonder where the cheese crackers is."

Ryan wondered the same thing. Getting to his feet, he went into the kitchen to check on Ivy and found her standing with both hands braced against the counter, her head bowed and tears dripping from her face. The box of crackers sat on the counter behind her. Working quickly, Ryan opened a cabinet above her head, took down two plastic bowls and filled them with small orange-colored crackers; he then carried them into the living room for the boys. He returned to guide Ivy over to the table, which consisted of a rectangular oak top mounted to four black legs. Pushing her down onto a matching chair, he handed her a paper napkin. She dutifully mopped her face, but then she just sat there, looking utterly dejected.

Ryan rummaged around until he found the coffee. Then he filled the pot, took down some mugs from the cabinet and went over to grip her shoulder with his hand. "Want anything with your coffee? Something to eat maybe?"

She shook her head. He sat next to her with his arms folded against the tabletop until the coffee was made. After filling a cup, he carried it back to the table and literally wrapped both of her hands around it. Without so much as glancing up, she lifted it to her lips and took a sip. He drank his own mug while quietly making telephone calls.

The first order of business seemed to be freeing himself for the evening. He called other coaches to cover practice and the principal, Kenneth Spicer, to manage his last class and the Honor Society meeting that evening. After accomplishing that task to his satisfaction, he went back into the living room and questioned the kids about what they might like for dinner. He followed with a call to the café downtown. Assured that four hamburgers with all the trimmings would be waiting when he went to pick them up at half-past five, he turned his full attention back to Ivy. They had almost three hours for Ivy to pull herself together well enough for him to feel comfortable about leaving her alone with the boys again.

Much the same way that he forced the cooperation of headstrong teenagers, he calmly bullied her into taking a nap, going so far as to walk her down a second narrow hallway, this one running the length of the house, to the room where she'd spent the night and making her lie down. When he covered her with the blanket folded across the foot of the narrow bed, she turned onto her side, tucked her hands beneath her cheek and wearily mumbled, "Thank you, Ryan. I'll never forget this."

"I just hope the coffee won't keep you from resting," he said, but her eyelids were already drifting closed. He went out and shut the door behind him.

Two hours later when he slipped back in to gently shake her awake, she sat straight up and looked at him with clear eyes, asking, "Are the boys okay?"

"I left them playing in their room."

"They've been so quiet all day." She got up and started making herself presentable, smoothing her tailored shirt before reaching up to pull the rubber band from her hair.

"Kids know," he told her. "I always did. I always knew when my mother was sad. Which was often."

"That must have been difficult," Ivy murmured, gathering her hair into her hands to put it up again.

"Very. Today I suppose she'd be on antidepressants or some other medication."

Ivy stopped what she was doing, and dark, silky tresses slid free to tumble about her face. "I'm so sorry."

"Not your fault," he said, taking the elastic band from her hand and gathering up her hair himself. She went stone still. "I've done this for my sister more times than I can count," he told her, manipulating the glossy strands and the elastic band. "Wait one minute."

Seconds later the ponytail swung smoothly against the back of her head.

Turning, she offered him a tremulous smile. "Thank you."

From habit—he assured himself that it was from habit—he kissed the top of her head. "My pleasure. Will you and the boys be all right if I go out long enough to pick up dinner?"

"Yes, of course, but you don't have to do that. I've taken enough of your time."

"Be back in a few," he said, cutting off further protest.

He left her standing there, one hand fingering her ponytail thoughtfully, and despite his fears and misgivings, he had to admit that being around Ivy just felt right. Maybe that's what scared him the most.

Ivy perched on the edge of the tub, watching in bemusement as the boys played submarine war with two red plastic ducks, a squeaky pig and a screw-on bottle cap.

"Boys will be boys," Ryan commented from the doorway. "You can give them ducks and pigs to play with, but they'll just use them as weapons and blow them up. Figuratively speaking, of course."

It appeared that he was right. She suspected Ryan Jefford usually was. Her guilt at having imposed on him resurfaced, as it had done throughout dinner and the early evening.

"You don't have to stay," she told him, hoping that he couldn't tell how much just the sight of him standing there filling up the doorway comforted her.

"Don't have anywhere else to be at the moment," he told her, looking somewhat surprised by that fact.

Selfishly, she did not try to convince him to go. Instead, she broke eye contact and concentrated on the boys, knowing that if she gave herself too much time to think regret would reduce her to tears again.

No one had to tell her that she had overreacted today, that her grief was out of proportion to her sister's loss. Likewise, no one had to tell her why. That did not make it any easier to bear, however. She wished that she could share the original source of her pain with Ryan. The more time she spent with him, the more she wanted to trust him with the details of her past, but she was afraid of how he might react. Would he look at her with disappointment? Scorn?

She let the boys play until the water in the tub cooled. "Time to get out, guys."

"A-w-w."

"Five more minutes," Hunter pleaded.

"Sorry. You're shivering now. Time to get dried off."

She leaned over and lifted the plug. Ryan crowded into the small room and pulled a towel from the bar beside the sink, holding it out to her. She wrapped the towel around Scott's shoulders and lifted him out just as Ryan came forward with a second towel and captured Hunter with it. They carried the boys to their bedroom, where Ivy had earlier laid out pajamas.

Some playful tussling later, they had both little bodies dried, dressed, teeth brushed and tucked into their twin beds. To her surprise, they did not insist on stories or books or bedtime games, but when Ryan suggested a prayer, both boys instantly stilled and pressed their hands together.

Ryan rose to stand between their beds, and when Ivy also stood, he moved behind her and lightly clasped the tops of her shoulders. Ivy bowed her head, feeling peace steal over her as Ryan spoke.

"Heavenly Father, we know that even when You allow sadness into our lives, You still love us. The quiet joy of Your love is always with us, and we thank You for that. Heal our hearts, Lord, and keep us safe as we go through this night and the days to come. Amen."

Ivy kissed the boys, told them good-night and then followed Ryan to the door. He shut off the overhead light, waited a moment as the night-lights blinked on and the boys snuggled down, then gently closed the door and walked Ivy through the hall, his hand riding lightly against the small of her back. She knew then what she wanted to do, needed to do. She owed it to him in some way. She would tell him the truth.

As soon as they entered the family room, she turned to face him.

"You've been so wonderful today, Ryan. I shudder to think what I would have done without you."

"I'm glad I could help."

"Do you have a few more minutes?"

A gentle smile twitched at his lips. "Like I said, I don't have anywhere else to be. For once."

Ducking her head, she folded her arms, surprised by an impulse to hug him. Instead, she swung away and dropped down onto the sofa. He followed suit, but this time, she noted, he left a good deal of space between them. That somehow felt awkward, and Ivy struggled to know where to start.

"You strike me as a very busy man," she said, knowing that she was avoiding the real subject.

He nodded slowly. "Everyone thinks teachers have it easy because they get several weeks off in the summer, but we pay for that time with long hours the rest of the year."

"What is it you teach again?"

"History. All of it. State history, American history, world history."

"And you're a coach? Football, isn't it?"

"Mostly. It's the assistant principal thing that really grabs the time, though. All those meetings and administrative duties and just the oversight, those pesky extracurricular activities that take up so many evenings."

"You love it, though, I can tell."

He flashed her a grin. "Yeah, I do. It's a calling. It's what I'm made for, meant for."

"I envy you that," she told him. "I fell into radio while studying for a communications degree in college. Don't get me wrong, I enjoy the microphone, and I've had a certain success with it, but it's come at a high price."

"How so?"

Still she hedged. "It's a tough gig, up one day, down another, and you're only as good as your latest ratings in your market and demographic. You move from market to market and format to format, hoping for the numbers to make national syndication. Every time you move, you leave something or someone behind."

He tilted his head, and she knew that the moment had come even before he gently asked, "What did you leave behind, Ivy?"

"Everything," she said around the lump in her throat. "Everyone."

They both knew that was not a full answer. He just sat there, waiting, until she told him. Strangely, though it was the first time she had ever spoken the words aloud, they proved less difficult to say than she had imagined they might.

"My daughter. I left behind…I *gave up* my daughter."

Chapter Eight

Everything inside Ryan's chest seized. For a moment, he seemed unable to breath or even swallow. Meanwhile, Ivy went on in a soft, tremulous voice.

"Her name is Chelsea. She's six. She and her adoptive family live in Seattle."

Ryan finally gulped down the clog in his throat. "I—I had no idea."

Ivy smiled wanly at that. "No one does. Only my family. And Brand, of course."

"Brand?"

"Her father." She looked away. "Or her sperm donor, as he calls himself."

"Sounds like a charming character," Ryan muttered, shocked to hear Ivy chuckle.

"You have no idea. When he wants to be, Brand Phillips is the most charming man in the world. Also the most selfish."

Brand Phillips. Ryan recognized the name. Ivy's partner on the controversial *FireBrand Phillips and Ivy* show. No wonder they broke up.

"Am I to take it that you had a child together but never married?" he asked carefully, dreading the answer. It would explain a lot, he thought, *hurt*, somehow, as odd as that seemed. She was none of his concern, after all, but that didn't seem to make any difference. He waited for her answer with a painfully thudding heart.

Her forehead wrinkled. "Something like that. I had a child, and no, we never married. We lived together for several years before I accidentally became pregnant, and when I refused to have an abortion, Brand left me."

"This was how long ago?" Ryan asked, confused.

"Six years, six months and seventeen days ago."

Ryan shook his head, more confused than ever. "But you continued your show together?"

"Eventually. After I gave up the baby for adoption, Brand came back. He convinced me that he loved me, so in a way we picked up where we'd left off."

Ryan could only stare at her. "Then why, Ivy? Why give up your child?"

Twisting sideways, she lifted a hand to cradle her temple, her elbow sunk into the back cushion of the couch. "When I signed the papers, I really didn't have any other choice. Brand broke up the act when he left, so I didn't have any means of support. I came back to Eden in hopes that my father would help me get on my feet, but…"

"He turned you away," Ryan surmised sourly.

Ivy sighed, nodding. "He had never approved of my relationship with Brand, never approved of my lifestyle. I was an embarrassment to him. He told me that I would be a terrible mother, and he was probably right." She looked straight at Ryan. "No, he *was* right. I was a mess."

"Still, Ivy," Ryan argued, "you were pregnant, alone and unemployed."

"And confused," she added. "I couldn't believe what I'd done to myself, what I'd done to my child. To that point, I had truly loved Brand, admired him, even, for what I saw as his courageous social convictions."

"Such as?"

"The 'battle against the norm,' as he called it, the right to dissent, to say outrageous things and defy social conventions."

"Like marriage and parenthood."

"Yes, like those, but other things, as well. Brand believes that because there are so many choices when it comes to religion, religion itself must be false and even harmful. He truly believes that religion is a shackle which humankind must throw off if we are to achieve true peace. Believing that, there is no convention or social ethic that he won't challenge."

"And you bought that?"

"I tried to, but when it came to aborting my child, I couldn't do what he asked. I simply could not. So I did the only thing I could see to do."

"You gave her up for adoption."

Ivy bowed her head, saying softly, "I've never seen her, not even a picture of her, since the day she was born. They've offered, her parents. They write newsy letters and cards a few times a year, usually for her birthday in August and again at Christmas, and I've kept them apprised of every change of address I've made, but I just don't think I can handle seeing her." Ivy began to weep then, not the great, horrible sobs of earlier, but a gentle stream of tears that washed her already scrubbed cheeks. "That's why I fell apart earlier. The loss of Rose's daughter felt in some way like my own loss all over again. Wow, it feels so good to talk about her!"

"You should be able to talk about her anytime you want," Ryan declared, reaching out to squeeze her hand. "You did a brave, selfless thing, Ivy. Be proud of that."

Ivy wiped her eyes, saying, "I made sure she had a good family, good parents who could give her everything I couldn't. A real home. Big sister. Financial security. A dad, grandparents, the works. And when it was too late to stop it, Brand came back."

"Ivy, how could you take him back after that?"

"I didn't have anyone else," she pointed out,

sounding somewhat desperate for him to understand. "My father wouldn't speak to me, told me never to contact him again. It had been years since I'd lived anyplace long enough to really make friends, and I was such a wreck after the baby was born. Brand took care of me until I could cope again, and I convinced myself that he truly loved me. I think I had to believe it. I found out later that we'd been offered a national syndication deal and that he needed me as part of the team to get it."

"Oh, yeah, that sounds like a courageous social hero, all right," Ryan sniped sarcastically. "He's willing to challenge all the social norms except those about making money."

"You don't know how right you are. When the contract offer first came to light, it seemed like such a stroke of luck. But I couldn't help thinking that if it had only come before I signed those adoption papers, I wouldn't have had to give her up. I wanted to reclaim her. We fought about it endlessly. And then it was just too late."

"But you stayed together?"

"More or less. I could never get over my resentment. For a long time, I just went through the motions to keep the peace, while Brand became ever more outrageous on air to keep the ratings up and the money coming in. The whole thing became a terrible, sick parody. I knew he played around, cheated on me. It didn't seem to matter. That's just

Brand, his cynical, self-centered view of the world, and we hadn't been anything more than roommates for a long time by then." She shook her head. "It all used to sound so exciting, back when I was young and stupid. The tripe he spewed about marriage being antithetical to human nature actually made sense to me at one time."

"With your parents to go by, I'm not surprised," Ryan muttered. Then he realized what he had said and sat up a little straighter. "Oh, I'm sorry. I shouldn't have said that."

"No, it's perfectly true," she insisted. "Everyone in Eden knew that my mother cheated on my father as casually as she waved at our neighbors in the street. Why he put up with it as long as he did, I'll never understand. I was about eleven when she took off the last time. After a while when he realized she wouldn't be back, he divorced her, and that was that."

"I think that must be when I really came to know your dad," Ryan mused.

"That's because he started going to church then," Ivy said. "But his religion didn't seem to lessen his bitterness. Rather, it seemed to increase it, as if it made her even more wrong and forgiveness was impossible. By the time I met Brand in college, I wanted nothing to do with my father's *religion*. Then a few months ago I met someone who made me see that it isn't about *religion*. It's about Jesus and what happened on that cross."

Ryan smiled, relieved to the soles of his feet. "I am so glad to hear you say that."

Ivy laughed, actually laughed. "I may have messed up my life, but at least I found my soul. You can't know how rich forgiveness really is," she went on, "unless you've sinned, really sinned, against God. For all that, though, I pray no one ever makes the mistakes that I have. Does that make sense?"

Ryan nodded. "I think so."

"Once I had made my peace with God," she said gently, "I could no longer live the lie."

"What happened?"

"Just what you'd expect. Brand told me in lurid detail what an idiot I am. To his way of thinking, everyone in the world is an idiot except him. He derided every tenet of Christianity, and ultimately offered me a choice."

"The same as before, I take it; his way or the highway."

"And I chose the highway, literally. He chose the divorced receptionist at the radio station in Tulsa where we were working," she added wryly, eyebrows raised. "Apparently she was smarter than me. He married her before I could get my stuff out of the apartment."

"Oh, Ivy. How awful for you."

"Humiliating, frankly."

"You must hate him," Ryan whispered. He knew

without a doubt that in her position that was how he would feel.

"I pity him," she said. "I wish him well. Truly I do. As impossible as it seems now, I loved him once, and I don't blame him for my mistakes. I should have known better. The truth is, I did know better, and eventually I couldn't outrun that fact anymore. Now all I care about is trying to make up for some of the damage I've done."

"That's why you came home," Ryan realized, somewhat humbled by her attitude.

"Yes."

Ryan thought of Olie and the ugly, bitter, judgmental attitude about his own daughter. He couldn't imagine his father or grandfather doing any of the things Olie had done, regardless of the circumstances. "I'm so sorry that your father hasn't welcomed you as you'd hoped."

"It's important that I reach out, but I can only do my own part and let Dad do his," she said. "I'm terribly thankful for Rose and that I could be here for her and the boys. I'm just so sad that she's had to go through losing a child." Tearing up again, she croaked out, "Oh, Ryan, there's no other pain like that. None."

He understood now how Ivy had suffered. For her, Rose's loss was like giving up her own daughter all over again. He saw, too, that she had risked, and received, her father's rejection for a second time. Some in town might condemn Ivy for her past, but he could only admire her courage, which he found somewhat unsettling. Glancing at his watch, he rose to leave.

"I'm sorry, but I have to go," he told her.

"I understand." She got up, and together they walked toward the front door. "Thank you, Ryan. For everything."

"You're very brave to have faced your mistakes, Ivy. I want you to know how much I admire your courage."

"And I want you to know how much I admire all of the Jeffords. Honestly, Ryan, I was terribly confused for a very long time about what the church actually taught, but whenever I thought of what Christians ought to be, I always thought of your family. You've shown me how right I was to choose that example for myself."

He blushed. Working around teenagers for so long, he thought he had forgotten how, but the heat that crept up his throat and burst into his cheeks proved otherwise. Before he could formulate a gracious reply to that very fine and probably undeserved, at least on his part, compliment, she opened the door and walked him outside.

"I'll be leaving Eden as soon as my sister is well enough to take care of her boys," she revealed. "So, have a wonderful life, Ryan, and thank you again." Framing his face with her cool, slender hands, she stretched up and tenderly kissed him on the lips. "Goodbye."

With that, she went back inside, but her light kiss had so stunned him that he couldn't be sure. He stood there like a dummy until the sound of a dog barking in the next-door neighbor's yard finally brought him back to his senses.

Troubled by his own visceral reaction to that light, friendly kiss, he turned and tramped to his car, telling himself that Ivy's leaving would no doubt be a good thing for him personally. So why then, he wondered, did he feel not one iota of relief at the thought?

The following Friday, Ivy let herself into the bland, impersonal motel room and tossed her bags onto the foot of the bed. It had broken her heart to see Rose return home with empty arms. Thank God for the boys. Their delight in welcoming their parents back and their obvious reluctance in letting their aunt go had made both the homecoming and the leave-taking easier.

Ivy hadn't known what she was getting into when she'd agreed to stay at the house and take care of those two little scamps. She had been shocked more than once over the past few days, but she smiled now to think of the time they had shared. Hunter and Scott had given her a taste of what she'd missed out on with her daughter, but all in all it had been a positive experience for her. She would no longer view every child as a breathing reminder of her own loss.

Rose had looked puffy and pale and on the knife-edge of her composure. Daniel hadn't had two words to say to Ivy herself, but his attentiveness to his family had warmed her. After settling Rose in their bed, he had taken the boys off to play so that she and Ivy could have some time together. They had held each other and wept while talking softly about all that had happened.

It had hurt Ivy to have to tell Rose that she couldn't attend the baby's memorial service the next afternoon, but it was for the best. Their father would, should, be there, and even the small service that her sister and brother-in-law had planned was no place for the confrontation Olie would surely force. Rose understood that, of course, but naturally she wished it might be otherwise.

Dan hadn't seemed pleased to find his wife weeping when he'd finally come back into the master bedroom to check on her, and his expression of gratitude to Ivy had sounded more like a dismissal than anything else, but Ivy couldn't blame him. She agreed that the family should get back to normal as quickly as possible. Despite Rose's weak protests, Ivy had gathered her things, kissed the boys and come back here to the Heavenly Arms to try to rest.

Suddenly chilled and anything but restful, she folded her arms and glanced around the room. With its plain beige walls, boxy, outdated furniture bolted in place and the dark, heavy drapes covering the only window, the place felt rather dreary. Lonely.

She wondered what Ryan might be doing, but quickly turned off that train of thought. She very much feared that she had begun to care for him more than was wise. Besides, they had already said their good-byes. She probably would not see him again.

A glance at the radio clock on the beside table told her that she had hours yet before she had to think of dinner. Determined to be optimistic, she told herself that it was not too late to call the radio station in Oklahoma City and check on that job. Best do it now before the weekend.

Going to her briefcase, she took out her electronic organizer and looked up the number. Then she sat down on the edge of the bed, picked up the telephone receiver and prepared to be disappointed. Twenty minutes later, she fell back on the bed and smiled up at the ceiling.

"Thank You, Lord God. Thank You."

The job was hers. Time to begin her new life. She could head up to the city tomorrow. She could sleep late and take her time. The drive wouldn't take more than two or three hours, and she didn't have to report to the station before Monday morning.

Maybe she would see Ryan again, be able to thank him for his kindness once more.

She tried to put thoughts of him away, aware of a tenderness toward him that she had no right to feel. After the life she had led, a kind, upright, responsible man like Ryan could never truly care for her. Could he? She thought of Matthew Barston and the great love that he bore Devony. But no, what Matthew and Devony had was truly special and extremely rare.

With great determination, Ivy turned her focus to the future. If God willed it, she would be on the air a week from the coming Monday.

But she would still be alone.

Wrong again, she told herself, smiling. Perhaps, Ivy mused, that had once been the case; she just hadn't had sense enough to know it before Devony had come on the *FireBrand Phillips and Ivy* show. Hearing Devony tell of the peace that Christ's love had brought her had changed Ivy forever. As Devony would say, no one who carried the Spirit of the living Christ in her heart could ever truly be alone.

Ryan rang the doorbell, remembering the last time he stood on this porch and the kiss that had rocked his world. Heat enveloped him, but it had nothing whatsoever to do with the hot, heavy glass casserole dish in his hands. When Daniel opened the door, Ryan felt both relief and disappointment.

"My sister-in-law, Cara, asked me to bring this by," he said, proffering the casserole. "All of our condolences come with it, of course."

Dan smiled wanly. "Thanks. Just bring it through here."

They walked into the family room, Ryan carrying the casserole by folded dish towels at each end. The boys lolled on their bellies on the floor, playing a board game of some sort, while their mother reclined on the sofa. Hunter's head popped up, and his face split into a wide smile.

"Mr. Jeffer!"

"Who's winning?"

"Me!" he crowed.

"Uh-uh, me!" Scott argued, coming up onto his knees.

"So it's a draw, huh?"

"What's a draw?" Scott asked, wrinkling his nose.

"A tie, honey," Rose explained, starting to sit up. "Hello, Ryan. It's good to see you."

"You stay just as you are," he told her, even as Dan came forward to take the casserole. "Careful. It's hot out of the oven."

Rose ignored him, swinging her legs off the sofa, blankets and all. She patted the cushion next to her, saying, "Sit, please. I want a chance to thank you."

"No need for that," he insisted, sinking down on the very edge of the cushion so she wouldn't have to look up at him. "I'm sorry I couldn't do more."

"No, no," she said. "How could you possibly have done more? It wasn't just getting us to the hospital. The boys and Ivy have told us all you did for them. We are so very grateful."

"I'm glad to have been of help," he said. "I'm just so sorry for all you've been through."

Her eyes filled. "Thank you. Please continue to pray for us."

"Absolutely." Hoping to change the subject, he glanced around, but the only topic that came to mind was Ivy. Finally, he came right out and asked. "Is Ivy around? I didn't see the hybrid when I was at the motel earlier." He hadn't seen it out front, either, but Cara had said she had not checked out yet.

Rose shook her head. "No, I'm afraid not. She's too afraid of running into Dad."

Ryan let that pass. The last thing Rose needed to be concerned about right now was her father's behavior.

"We won't have to cook for a week," Daniel announced, coming back into the room, "which is good since my kitchen skills stop at being able to operate a can opener."

"One of the benefits of living in a small town, I suppose," Ryan said. "Folks aren't too busy to stop to help." With that, he rose to go, but Rose reached out and snagged his hand. He sank back down.

"I hate to ask this," she said, "after all you've done, but could you do one more favor?"

"Rose," Daniel said, his tone part censure but mostly concern.

"We're having a small, private memorial service for the baby late tomorrow afternoon," she rushed on, keeping her voice low. "If you could persuade Ivy to come, it would mean so much to me."

"Honey, you know that's not wise," Daniel said, sitting beside her to wrap his arm around her shoulders. "Ivy and your father can't be trusted in the same place together, you know that."

Ryan bit his tongue to keep from correcting Dan. As far as he had seen, the only one who couldn't be trusted was Olie, but again, Rose didn't need to worry about that.

"Please, Danny," she whispered. "She's my sister, and she's grieving just like the rest of us. I can't let her go without knowing she'll be all right."

He didn't know where it came from, but suddenly Ryan heard himself proposing a solution, one that would address both Daniel's very justified concern and Rose's very understandable need. "I'll speak to Ivy," he said, "but it might be wiser if she came after the service or at least remained out of sight."

"That could work," Rose agreed. "Dan, you can ask Dad to go pick up the boys at your cousin's after the service and meet us here at the house afterward. That would give Ivy and me some time alone together in the chapel."

Dan nodded reluctantly. "But if something goes wrong and Olie refuses to cooperate—"

"He won't," Rose insisted. "I'll speak to Pastor Latimer myself so if Ryan can just convince Ivy…"

Ryan suddenly wished he'd kept his mouth shut, but he could not deny that he was glad to have a reason to see Ivy again. Perhaps it was foolish. Nothing, after all, could come of it. Even if Ivy had not been about to start a new life in Oklahoma City, they could have no future together. Not only was he too busy, too dedicated to his work, he was not ready to trust his heart to anyone and doubted he ever would be. Nevertheless, he would see Ivy and try to convince her to attend the service, although it meant saying goodbye to her again.

"I'll do my best," he told Rose, because that's what a Jefford always did. And because he wanted to see Ivy again, no matter the reason.

Chapter Nine

"So," Ryan said to his grandfather, wrapping up his story, "I have to speak to Ivy when she comes in."

Hap rocked in his great oak chair, contemplating the black pot-bellied stove in the corner of the front room, before commenting. "You don't seem too keen on it."

Sighing, Ryan sat forward on the black leather couch and pushed a hand through his hair. "I admire Ivy. She's made some mistakes, sure, but she's faced up to them, and she's paid big-time along the way. I think it must be God's will that she make peace with her father, for Olie's sake as much as hers."

"But?" Hap pressed.

"But." Ryan spread his hands. "I'm feeling a little overwhelmed, I guess. I mean, you know how demanding my job is, and then there's this thing with Matt Barston."

Hap grunted. They had discussed Matt's situation in detail, and Hap had advised Ryan to speak to Matt and get his side of the story, but when Ryan had admitted that he remained uncomfortable with that idea, Hap had advised him to continue to pray about the situation.

"And you really think that befriending Ivy is too great a risk for you to take?" Hap asked. "Is that it?"

Ryan squirmed. "Not befriending her, no, but she's at least peripherally involved in Matt's situation, and it just doesn't seem wise to get in deeper than I already am." He winced, hoping that didn't sound as self-righteous as he feared it did.

"Ah," Hap said. "I think I'm finally getting it. Your problem is that you already have feelings for the girl."

"I don't have feelings for her!" Ryan retorted, more forcefully than he'd intended. "Not like you mean. I—I hardly know her now. She's…" Beautiful. Wounded. Heartbreakingly brave. He gulped and slumped forward. "Besides, what difference does it make? She'll soon be gone again."

"So all you're worried about is a bit of gossip?" Hap mused.

"Well, of course, I'm worried about gossip," Ryan admitted. "Scandal is never a good thing for someone in my position. Just look at Matt."

"Hmm," Hap said, just that.

Ryan rushed on. "I mean, I feel sorry for Matt, and I want to help him."

Hap nodded. "I'd expect no less of you."

Ryan gulped. "As for Ivy and the Halseys, the whole thing is heartbreaking, and I'm obviously in the middle for a reason, so I'll do whatever is needed, whatever God wills. I just can't help thinking that I ought to be careful, all things considered."

Hap said nothing for several moments, but Ryan could sense that his grandfather did not entirely agree with his assessment of the situation. It was then Ryan realized that he had come seeking Hap's approval for his reticence in getting involved with both situations. He wanted Hap to tell him that he was right to keep his distance from both Ivy and Matt. What, Ryan wondered, did that say about him? Was Hap right that his budding feelings for Ivy scared him? And what about Matt? What was he supposed to do there? Confused, Ryan scrubbed his hands over his face.

"Well, you won't have to wait much longer to talk to Ivy," Hap informed him. "She told Cara earlier that she was running up to Waurika for something to eat. Ought to be back soon."

"She told Cara this when?"

"When Cara and Holt invited her to join them for catfish at the Watermelon Patch."

Ryan grimaced. Every other Friday Holt took Hap out to dinner while Ryan or Cara watched the motel desk. This was not Hap's usual Friday out, which might explain why Cara and Holt had invited Ivy to join them—especially as they'd invited Ryan, to join them, too. He'd begged off because he had to finalize next year's football schedule, so Cara had asked him instead to come by the motel when he'd finished, get the casserole out of the oven and deliver it to the Halseys. Obviously, Cara and Holt were doing everything they could to throw him together with Ivy. What was it about married people that made them try to pair up everyone else?

He tried to feel outraged but only felt confused and almost regretful, which made no sense because, any feelings aside, Ivy was about to leave again for good. Surely anyone who looked at this situation clearly would see that was for the best. Getting roped into an unwise romance would be foolish. Matt's situation proved that point. Right?

Just then, Ivy's boxy little hybrid turned off the highway and into the motel lot. Ryan welcomed the sight, visible through the large picture window in the outside wall, with equal amounts of relief and dread. With a quick prayer for guidance, he thanked his grandfather and hurried out to fulfill his promise to Rose.

Plucking the room key from the outside pocket of her fashionably oversized handbag, Ivy reached toward the lock in the door, only to turn away when Ryan called her name. She watched him jog toward her in the muted light cast across the motel lot from fixtures atop a pair of tall poles. Dressed in jeans, athletic shoes and a light orange polo shirt beneath a jean jacket, he looked fit and fine, a big, solid, handsome man, supremely comfortable in his own skin, and she felt an unwelcome yearning. Why hadn't she wound up with a man like this instead of Brand Phillips? Shaking her head, she admitted to herself that she had not even known that men like Ryan existed.

He drew up, smiling at her. "How was your dinner?"

She shrugged. "A sandwich is a sandwich."

"Yeah, I know what you mean. I had bologna and crackers at my desk myself."

They stood in silence for a moment, Ryan lifted a hand to the back of his neck, his face half in shadow. "I was over at Rose and Dan's earlier."

Sobering instantly, Ivy bowed her head. "How is she?"

"Emotional. Worried."

"Worried about what?"

"You. Basically, Rose wants you to come to the memorial service. She needs you, and she's concerned that you aren't properly dealing with your grief. I suspect that she fears that her loss has brought up old feelings having to do with the adoption."

Ivy blinked. She had never discussed her daughter with Rose. "Did she say that?"

"No, of course not. I assume that she doesn't know you've told me about Chelsea."

Ivy closed her eyes. That was the first time she had ever heard another person say her daughter's name, and just that was enough to make her eyes brim with tears.

"I think she's right," Ryan went on gently. "Obviously you need some sort of closure."

"There is no closure for this, Ryan."

"Perhaps not for Chelsea," he said, "but saying good-bye to Rose's child could help. Without that, Ivy, it seems to me you're carrying a double load of grief."

She shook her head. "Rose is the one who needs closure."

"True enough, and she needs you to be there with her when she says good-bye to her child," he argued.

Ivy sighed. She wanted that, too, but she could not risk it. She looked down at the keys in her hand and said, "I can't. My father will be at the service. He *should* be at the service. But you know what he thinks of me. He'll make a scene. I know he will. He won't be able to help himself."

"We thought of that," Ryan told her, explaining the plan. "Afterward, you and Rose can have some private time in the chapel together. She'll feel better about everything then, and so will you, I suspect."

Ivy sucked in a deep breath and lifted her head. "Maybe you're right."

"Then it's settled," he concluded, smiling. "I'll pick you up here about four."

She knew it was not wise for her to keep spending time with him. Nothing good could possibly come of it, especially considering that she was half in love with him already. Who wouldn't be? His kindness and sweetness alone would captivate most women. Add to that his innate goodness, compassion, strong sense of responsibility and masculine good looks, and she could not imagine what woman could resist him. Given her past, however, she was undoubtedly the last one whom he would, or ought to, consider. Yes, keeping her distance from here on out definitely made sense.

"You've done enough," she told him, "more than enough. I can get myself to the chapel."

"No doubt you can," he said, looking down so that his face was hidden in the inky shadow, "but I promised Rose."

Ivy bit her lip. She couldn't argue with that. Still, he had already done so much. "We seem to have dragged you into our problems, and I'm sorry about that."

"No, no. If I've been of some help," Ryan said. "I thank God."

"That makes two of us," she whispered. Stepping forward, she meant to lift up and kiss his cheek, but she instantly thought better of that. Remembering the unexpected charge that seemed to course between them the last time she had been so foolish, she stepped back nervously.

"Have a good evening," he said in an oddly thick voice before turning away.

She went inside, telling herself, *one more time*. She would see him one more time and then, very likely, never again, which would no doubt be the best thing, even if it gave her one more reason to grieve.

The small, closet-sized antechamber to the modest sanctuary inside the Magnolia Christian Church provided privacy and little else, with only a single folding chair, a pair of garment hooks on opposite walls and two mirrored doors, one in each end of the narrow room. Davis Latimer had escorted Ryan and Ivy there well before the service began, apologizing for the inconvenience. Ivy quite liked the young pastor, though she found his pale blue eyes somewhat disconcerting, as if he could see straight to the heart of a person. At Ryan's insistence, Ivy occupied the chair while he leaned against the wall, arms folded. In silence, they listened to the short, solemn ceremony.

For several minutes in the beginning, someone played soft piano music with surprising skill. Following this, the pastor read a passage of Scripture before an ethereal female voice sang a poignant song about joy in the presence of God. It was the same voice that had moved Ivy so at the Easter sunrise service. Ivy could hear sniffs and muffled sobs as the pastor briefly spoke about the hope and unrealized desire of the Halsey family to welcome a new member into its heart. With tears dripping from her chin, Ivy heard the name of her little niece for the first time, Angela Faith.

"An appropriate name for a precious child who will never know sin," the pastor said, "chosen by loving parents who dwell in the faith that the arms of the Savior will forever hold her close."

Ryan's strong hands gently gripped Ivy's shoulders. She closed her eyes, drawing strength from his comforting presence.

Pastor Latimer spoke for a few moments more about how God never promised us a pain-free existence or a life without disappointment. Rather, said the pastor, God pledged always to be with us, even when we railed against the unfairness and difficulties of this world, and to soothe our hurts in the hereafter.

The pastor closed the brief ceremony with prayer. Another instrumental piece followed. At length the music ended, and shuffling feet and murmurs could be heard. Finally, the door opened, and Ryan helped Ivy to her feet.

"Ms. Villard," Davis Latimer said. "If you'll come with me, I'll take you to your sister. Ryan, perhaps you'd best come, too. Rose is understandably distraught."

Ivy sent a despairing glance at Ryan, who clasped her hand with his. Together they followed Pastor Latimer from the tiny room and out into a small sanctuary fitted with dark gold carpet and pale oak pews set against bright white walls. They walked across the raised platform at the front of the church, passing the small grand piano where a thin blonde woman in silver, wire-rimmed glasses, whom Ivy recognized as Becca Inman, sat with folded hands. Before the simple oak altar at the front of the platform stood a bier draped in pink satin and holding a tiny white coffin bedecked with a single spray of pink rosebuds. Beyond this sat Rose in the front pew. As planned, Daniel had walked Olie out into the parking lot with instructions to pick up the boys from their cousin's house and take them home.

Rose reached up her arms as Ivy drew near, and they came together in a tearful embrace. Ryan slid into the pew behind them. Ivy barely noticed as the pastor slipped away.

"My beautiful little girl," Rose whispered, sobbing.

"I know, honey. I'm so sorry."

"Did you hear what we named her?"

"Angela Faith. Lovely, and so appropriate."

Rose drew back a little then, her brown eyes

strangely calm in her ravaged face. "I never knew," she said, "the name of your little girl."

Ivy felt her throat close. "Ch-Chelsea."

"Tell me about her," Rose insisted, laying her head upon Ivy's shoulder. "I was afraid to ask you before, but I've always wanted to know."

Ivy gasped a shuddering breath, but after a moment she began to speak, telling Rose, with tears and sniffles, everything she could about the niece whom Rose had never known. In the end, they were both somewhat calmer.

"So she's well and happy and loved," Rose concluded at last. "That must comfort you."

"It's all that's kept me sane," Ivy admitted.

Rose sat up and turned slightly to look her sister in the face. "We may not have our children with us, but my little one will never know a moment's pain, and yours will grow up knowing that she is wanted and loved."

Ivy managed to smile. "That's true. That's so true."

"I'm so glad you were here when this happened," Rose said, hugging her. "I thank God that I didn't have to go through this without you, and I'm so sorry that I wasn't there for you when you needed me."

Ivy framed her sister's beloved face with her hands. "No, no, that wasn't your fault. You didn't even know where to find me."

"All the same, I wish I'd been there." Rose

clasped Ivy's wrists. "If anything good has come of this, it's that I have my sister back."

"Rose."

"You have to promise me that we'll stay in touch," Rose said lowering both of their hands to her lap.

"Of course."

Rose shook Ivy's hands with hers. "And now that you're going to be living closer, we'll see more of you. Promise that you'll come next month for Hunter's birthday."

Ivy thought of her father and instinctively drew back. "Oh, honey, I don't know."

"Well, I do," Rose insisted. "It's the twenty-sixth, and that's a Saturday this year, a perfect time for celebration. Besides, I think we need a reason to celebrate, something to look forward to."

"Rose, you know how Dad feels."

"He'll just have to get over it," Rose decreed, "because I'm not giving up on this. Now say you'll come."

"We'll see," Ivy hedged. "I have to figure out how this new job is going to go before I make any promises." Rose frowned, but then, to Ivy's relief, she nodded.

"But don't think I'm going to forget about it," she warned.

Ivy smiled and laid her head against her sister's. "It's good to be wanted," she said. "I can't tell you how good it is to be wanted by someone."

"Oh, Ivy!" Rose exclaimed, wrapping her arms around her sister. "I'm so glad you came home."

Ivy closed her eyes, basking in the joy of her sister's love, but in her mind's eye she saw the anger and derision on their father's face. *He* was not happy that she had returned. Behind her, she heard Ryan shift on the pew, and she wondered what he thought about her coming home. He probably wished she had stayed away, too, and who could blame him? To her father she was an unwanted reminder of past shame, and to Ryan she had been nothing but trouble. Unfortunately, she did not see either circumstance changing. She could do nothing to remove the shame of her past, which meant that associating with her could do nothing good for Ryan. In truth, raising her sister's hopes was all she had succeeded in doing with her return.

Perhaps, she told herself, staying away might have been kinder to everyone.

In his thirty-four years, Ryan had attended more than his fair share of funerals, but nothing, not the passing of his grandpa Mike or the stunning dual loss of his parents, had moved him quite like the grief of Ivy and Rose. He had wanted to hold Ivy and protect her from her tears, which told him that he was much more deeply involved with her than he'd even realized. When Rose had asked Ivy to attend Hunter's birthday party next month, Ryan had waited with bated breath, both hoping and fearing that Ivy would agree. Instead, she had danced around the promise her sister asked of her, and it was that unmade promise that troubled him as he escorted Ivy from the church and drove her back to the motel.

"Once again, Ryan," she told him as they sat in his car in front of her room, "I am deeply indebted to you."

He shook his head. "I'm just sorry this all happened, the baby, your father, everything."

"Not everything," she said, smiling gently. "I've gotten to know you again."

Ryan gulped mentally. He knew that she expected him to say something to that. He even thought about saying that they were friends, brother and sister in Christ, but his tongue felt welded to the roof of his mouth. After a moment, she bowed her head and went on.

"Most importantly, I've reconnected with my sister and met my nephews. I have family again, Ryan. You cannot know what that means to me."

"Does that mean you'll be back in April for Hunter's birthday?" he managed to ask, desperate to know one way or another.

She sucked in a deep breath, as if she had to steel herself just to think about it. Part of him hoped she would say yes; part of him hoped not. Both told him that he would be wise to avoid her if she did return to town, that his feelings for Ivy were too tender, too…dangerous. At last, she shook her head.

"I just don't know."

The relief he had hoped for eluded him; a disappointment that he did not want to acknowledge rushed in instead. He fought it, telling himself that he had done his Christian duty by Ivy and her family, and now the time had come to permanently part ways with her. But she was so achingly beautiful and brave. Could it be possible that he really would not see her again?

She opened the door and got out.

"Take care of yourself," she said.

"You, too."

At the last moment, before the door closed, she fluttered a little wave at him, and something about that seemed so sad, so bereft, that it haunted him. Ryan sat for a long time after she'd gone into her room, dissatisfied with their parting but sure that it was for the best. Wasn't it?

Finally, he started the car and drove home without stopping in at his grandfather's apartment. He did not want to talk to Hap just now or anyone else, for that matter. Yet, when he arrived back at his place, he walked from room to room, on edge and uncertain why.

The large, airy chambers, arched doorways and multi-paned windows usually pleased him. Something about the solidity of the house itself, the heavy plaster moldings, the luster of the red oak floors, the warm, cozy elegance of the fireplaces and the enduring air of it all had always comforted him. But not today. For the first time his lovely old house felt cold and empty and bare. He wandered around the sparsely furnished rooms, noticing a problem here, a lacking there. For the first time, the house felt *almost* right, *not quite* complete. Something seemed missing, but he could not for the life of him imagine what.

He tried to ignore the feeling, sure that he simply wasn't used to having so much free time. Usually he would be designing teaching plans or chaperoning some student gathering or grading papers or… The list sometimes seemed endless, but now suddenly it also seemed trivial.

Sighing, he took himself into his neat, roomy kitchen and put together an early dinner of canned hash, canned green beans, canned carrots and saltine crackers, washing it all down with a canned cola in front of the television in the den next to his bedroom. Perhaps that was the problem, he mused, looking at the soda. Maybe, without his even realizing it, his whole life had been canned, neatly packed into a very small but somewhat flimsy container.

And maybe he was just in an odd mood because of the funeral today. Yes, that must be it. Surely, with a little time, this unsettled feeling would pass.

Not willing to seek out company but dissatisfied

with what he found on the TV, he picked up a novel he'd been meaning to read and carried it to bed with him. When he closed the covers, dawn was pushing back the night, and the problem that had niggled at him for hours burst fully realized into his mind.

Suddenly he knew that he should have stayed with Ivy yesterday or, better yet, kept her with him. He should have invited her out to dinner, should have taken her over to visit with Hap, anything instead of leaving her all alone after the funeral of her niece on her last night in town. He should have invited her to join the family for church this morning and dinner afterward. He should have honored her bravery with complete support. He should have prayed with her and for her and told her again how much he admired her determination to overcome her past and make up for her mistakes.

But he had done none of those things. He had not even prayed about his own troubling disquiet last night, for fear of what he might hear God telling him, of what he might learn about himself. What was he frightened of, that Ivy's past would somehow harm his position? Or of his feelings for her and what those feelings might do to his heart and his world?

Feeling small and foolish, he got up to make himself a pot of coffee. Then he sat on a stool at the old, scarred butcher-block island in his kitchen and apologized to God for being such a self-centered idiot.

"Forgive me, Father," he whispered after several minutes of intense prayer, "for letting my fear get the better of me. Why should I fear when You are with me? Show me what the right thing is and help me do it always. Amen."

He got up to shower, shave and make himself presentable before driving over to the motel early. He walked straight to Ivy's door, but after knocking for a good ten minutes, he had to accept the fact that she was not going to answer.

Trudging to the apartment, he let himself in through the back door and found Hap pouring milk over a bowl of cereal in the long, narrow kitchen.

"Well, good morning," Hap rasped. "You're getting around early. Want a bowl?"

Ryan shook his head. "Have you seen Ivy? She doesn't appear to be in her room."

"Ivy checked out around eight last evening, son," Hap told him.

Lurching sideways, Ryan slumped against the cold, metal, industrial grade countertop. She'd left not three hours after he had dropped her off.

"I thought you knew," Hap went on, brow furrowed. "She said she had to head to the city and get ready to start her new job."

Ryan shook his head. "No, I—I thought she'd wait until today."

Hap rubbed his hoary chin. "Guess that's why she left the envelope."

"Envelope?" Ryan straightened.

"On the counter in the front room," Hap said, nodding in that direction.

Ryan didn't wait for further explanation, just pushed past his grandfather and strode rapidly across the dingy dining room, past bedrooms and bath, to the lobby. Turning away from the sitting area, he went to the registration counter. There he found a plain white envelope with his name written on the front in neat, flowing script.

He lifted the flap, extracted a single folded sheet of lined paper and unfolded it.

"God bless you, my friend," it read. "Once more the Jeffords have shown me what following Christ truly means. Please keep an eye on my sister, Daniel and the boys, and thank you again for all that you've done to make this time easier for us. Ivy."

Ryan stared at the few words. They felt terribly like a final goodbye, as if she never expected to see Eden—or him—again.

He slid the paper back into the envelope and tucked it into his coat pocket, telling himself that this was his answer. Surely this was God's will and all for the best, but to his surprise he could not quite believe it.

Maybe, he admitted to himself, because he didn't really want to.

Chapter Ten

A male voice crooned and warbled in milky tones which surely owed as much to electronic manipulation as God-given talent, but Ryan did not get up and cross the room to change the dial of the small radio sitting on the sill of his office window, where the reception seemed best.

No, this was not about the music, this was about…Ryan really wasn't sure what this was about, frankly, but he'd been listening for the past week and a half, ever since Ivy's show had debuted on the first Monday in April. He had to admit that Ivy knew what to do with a microphone. She sounded as natural as if she were actually in the room with him but with a slight air of authority and expertise. This was an Ivy he'd never met, an Ivy he was growing to admire.

Kenneth Spicer, the high school principal and

Ryan's boss, opened the door and walked in. "Hey, Ryan, what do you think about this fund-raising request by the PTA?"

A short, stocky man with dark, thinning hair, Spicer was perhaps two decades older than Ryan. Pitching back in his chair, Ryan linked his hands behind his head and propped his feet on the near corner of his desk.

"I'm inclined to give it the go-ahead," Ryan said. "I don't know how many people will be interested in a public reading, but I happen to like Shakespeare myself, and it's apt to be as close to a real staging as we're likely to get around here. Could be fun."

"Could be dull as ditchwater, too, but I don't see what it can hurt to give them the theater for the evening." Spicer raised his brows. "If, that is, you're willing to act as auditor."

Ryan had begun to notice recently how often Spicer pushed off his responsibilities onto him, not that he minded particularly. Kenneth had a family at home, after all—well, a wife anyway, their children being grown now. Still, it seemed that Spicer often went home while he, Ryan, stayed behind to monitor some school function. Ryan almost refused this particular duty, just to let his superior know that he didn't like being taken advantage of, but then he thought better of it. One of them had to be there, or the school board would deny the use of the facility. Why shouldn't he audit the Shakespeare reading when he might enjoy it and Kenneth definitely would not?

"Okay. Fine."

Before Ryan finished speaking, the song playing on the radio ended and Ivy's familiar, throaty female voice came across the wire.

"This is *Ivy and Friends* in the one o'clock hour. Thank you for joining us. Today's theme is romance, just what every hardworking woman wants from her man, right, ladies? And who better to inspire us than our last artist? We'll be taking your calls after the break to discuss what women find romantic."

Spicer made a sound somewhere between a snort and a *humph,* hitching one hip up onto the far corner of Ryan's desk. "Romance. I can tell you what my wife finds romantic; my doing the dishes. At least that's what she claims."

Ryan chuckled. "Seems to work for my brother-in-law, Ty." Actually, the Jefford brothers had gotten a kick out of how often and eagerly one of the richest men in several states helped their sister clean her kitchen.

Sobering, Spicer nodded toward the radio, which was playing a commercial at the moment. "Is that the Ivy Villard show?"

"Yes, it is."

The principal gave his head a little sideways jerk. "You sure you ought to be listening to that here?"

"Why not?"

"Isn't it, you know, kind of racy?"

Ryan glanced at the radio, wondering what Kenneth had heard that he had not. "I don't think so. I certainly haven't heard anything I'd call racy."

"Well, it's just that her shows are always rather raunchy, aren't they? At least that's what I've heard. Actually," Kenneth muttered, "that's the least of what I've heard."

Ryan sat up abruptly, his feet hitting the floor. "What have you heard?"

Kenneth's smiled turned lascivious. "I, um, wouldn't want to repeat it, frankly." Then, of course, he did, ending with, "It was a regular orgy all the time, or so they say."

Unable to believe what he had just heard, Ryan got to his feet. Parking his hands at his waist, he twisted first one way, then another before declaring flatly, "I cannot believe you would actually repeat such a thing."

"Hey," Spicer said, his face coloring, "what's the big deal? It's just us guys."

"Yeah, what's a foul rumor between guys, especially when it's an outright lie?"

Kenneth slid off the corner of the desk. "How would you know that?"

Catching his temper by the merest edge, Ryan swallowed hard and tried to tame the lash of his voice. "I know Ivy. I know what she's been through and what she's done, and I admit that some of it I wouldn't have approved of, but there are chunks of my own life that, in hindsight, I can't approve of, either. What's more, I imagine if you're honest, you'd have to say the same thing. Everyone would, to some degree."

Principal Spicer frowned. "How is it that you know her so well?"

"She grew up here, same as me. And we had the chance to catch up with each other over Easter."

Kenneth Spicer shook his head. "I'm told this information came from her own family, and if you can't believe them, then who can you believe?"

Ryan caught his breath. It had to be Olie, of course, although how any father could do such a thing to his own daughter, Ryan did not know. To Principal Spicer he said, "In this case, I think you'll find that the source of this filthy rumor is one disgruntled family member and that the rest of the family vehemently disagrees. They, I believe, will stand by her. In fact, I'd stake my life on it."

"If you're not careful," Spicer muttered, heading for the door, "you could be staking your career on it." He turned at the last moment and shot a warning look at Ryan, saying, "You might want to think about which old friends you catch up with from now on."

Ryan stood there, rocked. Without the least warning, a savage anger roared through him. Unaccustomed as he was to such emotion, he didn't know what to do with it. He wanted to shake Kenneth Spicer until his teeth rattled.

Suddenly, Ryan remembered the seething, brittle edge that he had heard in Matt Barston's voice the last couple of times they'd talked, and understanding as clear as the anger abruptly swamped him. All at once, he knew exactly what Matt must be feeling. It was as if, in perfect hindsight, Ryan could identify Matt's every nuance of tone and gesture. Dropping into his chair, Ryan propped his chin against one upraised palm and ordered his rioting thoughts.

He still did not know how much of the gossip about Matt's wife was true, but he certainly knew now what righteous anger felt like. To have someone you cared about slandered in such a hateful, repugnant, even salacious manner when you knew the truth of the thing, was enough to…

Ryan sat back with a plop, his thoughts rewinding. Cared about? He gulped. Well, sure he cared about Ivy, he told himself. He cared about anyone who suffered unjustly, anyone at all.

But maybe he cared about Ivy a little more than he'd realized. He certainly cared about her more than he cared about her sister or her father or Matt and Devony Barston. Not that he didn't care about those people, of course, but with Ivy it was different. With Ivy it was somehow more intense, more *personal.*

Her voice came back on the radio. "Hello, this is Ivy. Thanks for calling. State your first name and, if you want, where you're from, then make your comment or ask your question."

"Yeah," said another female voice, "this is Lissa, and I have a question. My boyfriend's idea of romance is to go out with the boys, then show up at my place and fall into my bed. I've told him it ticks me off. I mean, what about a nice dinner or a movie first? But he keeps on doing it. How can I get him to stop?"

Ryan closed his eyes, moaning a silent prayer that Spicer was not listening to this. Seconds ticked by before Ivy said, "You kick him to the curb, that's how." As the caller sputtered about love and how guys will be guys, Ivy went on. "What he's doing to you is disrespectful, and you have to respect yourself before you can command a guy's respect. That means never going to the bedroom with some man who doesn't want you and respect you enough to put a ring on your finger *first*. When he wants and respects you enough to pledge his life and fidelity to you, *that's* real romance. That's how God designed the thing. Without that, all you've got is sex and being used. Believe me, I know what I'm talking about."

Sitting up quite straight now, Ryan snapped his jaw closed. As Ivy went to another music selection, he grinned.

"That's my girl," he said to the radio, and marveled at how much he suddenly wanted that to be true.

Now nobody could say that Ivy Villard did not stand on her convictions. She could have taken the easy way out just now, fallen back on old habits and expectations, embraced the modern culture and pleasure for its own sake. She could have even dismissed the whole thing, made light of it with a joke and hustled the caller off the air without taking a stand one way or another. Instead, she had said what needed to be said, and God bless her for it.

Ryan again thought of Matt. What a coward Ryan was not to stand up for an old friend he had always known to be an outspoken, upstanding Christian. Maybe he did not know Devony or her story, but he knew Matt. Had he even taken the time to discuss his concerns with his old buddy? No, he'd been too embarrassed even to broach the subject. Worse, had he so much as bothered to take a look at the Web site Matt had asked him to? He didn't even have a feeble excuse for that one.

Feeling like the worst heel, Ryan searched his desk for the slip of paper with that Web address on it. *Please, Lord*, he prayed, *don't let me have thrown it away*. Although he had no memory of stashing it there, he finally found the thing under the blotter. A few minutes later, he sat looking at photos of a private boarding school tucked into the hills north of Tulsa.

A Christian institution called The Moriah Academy for Boys, in reference to the area where God had led Abraham in order to test him with the commandment to sacrifice his son Isaac, the school operated entirely from donations and took only boys with troubled pasts seeking to "remake themselves as God wills." The institute boasted a long list of accomplishments backed up by testimonials, news accounts, facts and figures. A recent monetary gift had allowed the school to expand, and it sought Christian educators with "a heart for demonstrating God's forgiveness."

A heart for demonstrating God's forgiveness.

If that didn't describe Matt, Ryan didn't know what would.

He recalled an incident from their youth when Matt's gym locker had been mistaken for that of another boy by a group playing a destructive prank. They had soaked Matt's workout clothes in molasses, destroying some of his gear, which Matt's family could ill afford to replace, and booby trapped the locker with a balloon that exploded when the door was opened. A flying knot of rubber had nearly put out Matt's eye. It had lacerated his cheek and required stitches. The boy who had been the intended target of the prank had been so insulted that he had flown into a rage and knocked down two of the ringleaders.

Matt, with blood dripping off his chin, had

helped them both up, accepted their stammered apologies and been a perfect gentleman about the whole thing. Those two boys had later shown up at a church youth rally with Matt and were both now serving as deacons in the church.

How, Ryan asked himself, could he have forgotten that? The Matt he knew was a Christian strong enough to live what he believed, and that was what Ryan wrote about him now in the on-line recommendation form. He could only pray that it was not too late to do Matt some good.

Feeling better than he had in days, Ryan got off the computer and reached for the satellite phone that he carried in his jacket pocket. He dialed the number that he'd listened to Ivy give out repeatedly over the past three days, praying that he had enough time to get through before he had to teach his next class.

He quickly found that he had to turn off the radio in order to make a satisfactory connection, but he was able to listen to her field responses to the last segment of her show on the telephone. Some callers were derisive about the advice Ivy had given to Lissa, advising Ivy to "get real." Some were supportive. Nearly all were female. One male caller went off on Ivy about how women expected it all to be "one way," how they demanded romance, then left a fellow with nothing but bills. Ivy calmly told him how sorry she was for his bad experience and suggested that escaping such grasping females had been a blessing in disguise.

When Ivy announced that they only had time for a couple more calls, Ryan thought he might not get through, but then a voice informed him that he was next, and seconds later, Ivy said, "This is Ivy. Let's hear it before we have to go to break."

He floundered for a heartbeat, unsure if she actually meant him or not, but then he figured out he was on the air. "Uh, hi. This is Ryan, from Eden."

"Ryan!" she exclaimed. "Hey, thanks for calling!"

He smiled at the glad surprise in her tone. "Yeah, I just wanted to say that, as a guy, I totally agree with your answer to Lissa earlier."

"Did you hear that, ladies?" Ivy said. "There are still men in this world who want a woman who respects herself."

Ryan turned his chair around, putting his back to the door and went on. "Can I ask a question?"

"Sure."

"When are you planning to visit your alma mater again?"

The airwave transmitted an instant of silence before Ivy laughed. "Folks, you're listening to a proud graduate of Eden Memorial High. Unfortunately, I can't say when I might make it down your way again, Ryan, but tell everyone hello for me, will you?"

He fought down a spurt of disappointment. "I certainly will."

"Thanks again for calling," Ivy said, her voice noticeably softening, then the connection abruptly broke.

Ryan put away the phone and sat there for several seconds, ordering his mind for prayer. Finally, he bowed his head and pinched the bridge of his nose.

Thank You, Father God. I guess I've been careening around between fear and foolishness. I suspect that I sometimes think I know what's best when I haven't even bothered to ask the right questions. You've helped me see things a little clearer now. Just one thing more, Father, please stop these ugly rumors about Ivy from spreading. She's been hurt enough. These things I pray in the name of Your Holy Son, Jesus the Christ, my Lord and Savior. Amen.

After a long day of meetings and classes, followed by sports practice, Ryan was trying hard to resist his older brother's cajoling.

"Come on, little brother. Come out to dinner with us," Holt urged. "Granddad's got Teddy and Justus to keep him company."

"Besides," Charlotte added, hanging on her husband's arm, "when was the last time the Jefford kids all got to go out to dinner together?"

The last time was a week ago, when he had accompanied his brother and sister-in-law to the catfish joint outside of town. That had been the Friday after he had called in to Ivy's radio show. Among the crowded, packed dining halls of the tumbledown Watermelon Patch restaurant, talk had swirled that Ivy was "up to her old tricks" again. One grizzled old-timer had even stated that Ivy's show amounted to "sex on the air."

Ryan had felt compelled to put down his fork and ask if the fellow had ever actually listened to Ivy's show. When the older man admitted that he had not, Ryan had taken it upon himself to inform everyone within his hearing that Ivy's topics thus far had covered such things as marketing to females, balancing work with family, the nature of real romance, the best jobs for women and the worst excuses for everything from missing work to messing up the house. The man had given him a puzzled look and announced, "That's not what her own father says."

It had taken all of Ryan's self-control to reply that in this case Olie Villard was sadly mistaken. His appetite gone, he had calmly risen, swept the room with an icy glare and informed Holt and Cara that he needed a breath of fresh air and would be waiting in the truck. They had followed him out a short time later, but Ryan had been too angry to discuss the situation rationally just then.

In the week since, his anger had only grown, which was why he had not sought out Olie and taken him to task. He feared what he might do if Olie spewed more of his invective for Ivy at him. In fact, he did not think he had a good enough handle on his temper to discuss this issue with anyone still.

That being the case, Ryan knew that he had no business returning to the Watermelon Patch, which was the unofficial local gathering place, even if his sister and brother-in-law had come from Dallas for the weekend to visit and check on the house they were building.

"No, thanks," he said in reply to his brother's urging. "I'd just embarrass myself."

Holt crammed his new summer straw cowboy hat onto his head, grumbling, "Just because Olie showed up at prayer meeting again on Wednesday."

"He requested prayer that Ivy's show be 'stamped out,' Holt," Ryan snapped. "He knows there's nothing wrong with her show, but because callers keep bringing up topics that were covered by her former partner, Olie's telling everyone that some great evil's sprung up out of Eden. It's ridiculous."

"Granddad set him straight."

"You really think so? Are you telling me that the talk's died down?"

"I didn't say that," Holt muttered.

"I think it's awful what's being said about Ivy," Cara put in, "but what can we do except stand up for her?"

"Hard to stand up to her if you're hiding out," Charlotte said gently to Ryan.

"I'm not hiding out," Ryan insisted, "but I won't do Ivy any good if I lose my temper while defending her."

"That serious, is it?" Charlotte surmised, smiling wryly.

Ryan felt himself blush, but he brazened it out, pretending that he had missed her implication. "Yeah, it's that serious. It's worse than simply unfair, and I'm plenty ticked off about it. Makes my blood boil, to tell you the truth, and that's why I'm better off staying here trouncing this trio at dominoes."

He waved a hand at the three old men sitting around the game table in the motel lobby behind him. As expected, they hooted and launched a good-natured attack.

"You wish!"

"Can't trounce anyone without a partner, boy. Best remember that."

"Big talk. Now let's see you back it up."

"I'm coming, I'm coming," Ryan told them, shooing his siblings and their mates out the front door. "You four go on and have a good time. And don't worry about me."

"Wouldn't speak too soon if I were you," Hap

counseled, tongue in cheek, as the two couples disappeared from view. "You drew Justus for a partner tonight."

Chuckling, Ryan turned back to the table and resumed his chair. Teddy Booker, on Ryan's right, shook the dominoes then waited until the others had drawn seven each before raking in the left-overs.

Hap got the bid on that hand and called treys as trumps before running the table by winning all seven tricks.

"Should've bid two marks on that one," Teddy chuckled.

Ryan figured he might as well play his own game from then on and successfully outbid the others for the next two hands, making the first easily and the second by the skin of his teeth, thanks to the clever play of his partner. The fourth time around, Ryan got the bid again, paying a high price for it.

"Okay," he said, trying to figure out which of his dominoes to lead with, "let's see if Justus can keep me out of trouble."

"Son," Justus drawled, shifting sideways to dangle one arm over the back of his chair, "it's gonna take more than a crack Forty-Two player like me to keep you out of trouble."

"With these trumps you may be right," Ryan muttered, continuing to study his hand.

"I don't think he's talking about dominoes," Hap said, turning his playing tiles face up on the table.

Confused, Ryan looked to his grandfather. "What are you doing?"

These three played a cutthroat game, going so far as to force the bid on the dealer if the other three players passed ahead of him. They did not just lay down their dominoes.

Hap smiled, hung an elbow on the edge of the table and nodded toward the picture window. Ryan looked that way just in time to see Ivy reach toward the door. He was on his feet when she came through it.

A bright smile broke across her face, the dark ponytail on the back of her head swinging jauntily. She struck a pose, shoving her enormous handbag back and hooking her thumbs in the pockets of her slender denim capris, straining the fabric of her bright red T-shirt with its straight neckline and neat cap sleeves.

"Hey. My favorite caller!"

Ryan mirrored her pose. Tucking his thumbs into the back pockets of his jeans and pressing back his elbows, he winked. "Well, if it isn't my favorite radio host. Hey, yourself."

Ivy laughed. "Can a girl get a room around here?"

"Indeed, she can," Ryan declared. "You can fill out the registration card later."

"At least I have a proper address to put on it now," she said with a grin.

He could not quite believe how delighted he was to see her. After standing there for some seconds drinking in the sight of her, he suddenly realized that he was on the edge of making a spectacle of himself. With a jerk, he cast around for the next step to take, and it hit him when he glanced at the apartment door.

"Had your dinner by any chance?"

She shook her head, admitting, "No, I didn't want to stop until I got here."

"Ah. That would explain it then."

"What?" she asked, blinking at him.

"Why we have a pizza out there in the freezer with your name on it," he quipped, somehow managing to keep his tone and expression level. All three of the old men around the domino table chortled, even as Ryan asked, "Isn't that right, Granddad?"

"Sure enough," Hap confirmed. "Welcome home, Ivy."

"Thanks," she said, while Ryan stepped to her side. "It's good to be back."

Ryan swept out an arm and ushered her toward the apartment, saying, "Ma'am, your pizza awaits. A little help would sure speed things up, though."

"Of course," she replied brightly.

As Ryan hurried her away, he heard the dominoes clacking together behind them.

"Looks like it's plain old dominoes for us tonight," Teddy said.

"Yep," Hap confirmed.

"Okay by me," Justus retorted happily. "I can beat you two old softies at any game you choose."

Ryan looked down at Ivy, found his smile reflected there, and knew with a growing sense of alarm that he would do almost anything to keep her from hearing the lies being spread about her. He would, he realized, do almost anything to keep that smile on her beautiful face.

Chapter Eleven

Frozen pizza had never tasted so good. Ivy knew without a doubt that it had more to do with the company than the canned pineapple slices Ryan had insisted they add to the toppings before sliding the frozen pie into the oven, although she had to admit that the sweetness of the pineapple offset the spiciness of the pepperoni to perfection.

She felt quite sated, but that last slice was speaking to her. She reached across the oval maple table in the homey dining room of the motel apartment and, with a fork, cut off the tip of that last slice of pizza, which she then poked into her mouth.

Ryan sipped his soda and nodded toward the pizza pan. "Is that for me?"

"Mm-hm. If you don't eat it, I will, and then I'll pop."

He chuckled and reached for the last bit of the pizza, saying, "Can't have that. I like you unpopped."

Ivy put her head back and laughed. "Why is it," she asked, "that you suddenly seem so entertaining?"

"Nothing sudden about it. I've always been entertaining," he quipped. "You just haven't been around to enjoy my sparkling wit."

"And I thought you were so boring back in high school."

Ryan's eyebrows jumped up into his hairline. "Oh, really? Do tell."

Embarrassed, Ivy backpedaled a bit. "No, I just mean that, well, when I made the cheerleading team as a freshman, every other upper classman seemed to hit on me but you."

Ryan sat back in his chair, his hands resting on the edge of the tabletop. "Didn't think you noticed."

"I noticed," Ivy replied softly.

He sat forward again. "So did I. To tell you the truth, if I'd been just a year younger, I'd have been all over you, just like the other guys."

"Really?"

He nodded. "I was always very much aware of you, Ivy."

She tried not to let that feel too good. That was then. This was now, and too much water had passed under her bridge since then, but it helped to know that Ryan had been as aware of her as she had been of him. Still, she had to know something.

"Why didn't you ask me out, Ryan? Was it because of my mother?"

He seemed genuinely surprised. "Absolutely not. Why would you think that?"

Ivy spread her hands. "It was always that, in one way or another. Some of the boys asked me out because they thought I might be like her. Some kids avoided me for the same reason."

"Quite frankly, I never thought about your mom one way or the other. I won't say I wasn't aware of her reputation or that I haven't been a self-righteous prig at times," Ryan told her softly, "but back then I was simply focused on the future. You see, my dad really wanted his sons to go to college. He never did, and he always said that meant he had to make his living the hard way. He never talked about *if* we went to college, only *when* we went to college, so that became our focus, too."

"He must be very pleased with how you turned out," she said.

"I hope so." Ryan ducked his head, laced his fingers together atop the table and looked up at her. "Can I ask you something that's been bothering me?"

Mentally gulping, Ivy nodded. "Sure."

"How do you know Devony Barston?"

Ivy relaxed into a broad smile. "Devony is my spiritual mother, you might say."

"What?"

"It was Devony who led me to the Lord, Ryan."

He gaped at her. "We are talking about Matt Barston's wife, aren't we?"

Nodding, Ivy said, "She was Devony Pulen when I first came to know of her." Ivy went on to explain how she'd stumbled across Devony's Web site months earlier while surfing the net looking for subject matter for the *FireBrand Phillips and Ivy* show.

"Are you talking about the Web site with the photos?" Ryan asked haltingly.

"Photos? I don't know what photos you mean."

"I—I only know that there were some photos of Devony on the Internet recently."

"Well, the site I'm talking about is called Reclaiming Purity, and it's a counseling ministry."

"A counseling ministry?" he echoed, sounding confused.

"Exactly. Devony tells her personal story on the site and offers free online counseling to others trying to get out of that life. I assume you know that she was once a prostitute."

Ryan rubbed the back of his neck, nodding absently. "Maybe you better tell me Devony's story."

Ivy gladly did so. It wasn't a pretty story, but neither was it unique. At fourteen Devony had run away from her home in California to escape an abusive stepfather only to find herself on the streets in Los Angeles, where she was virtually kidnapped, raped, drugged and, once she was hooked, forced to prostitute herself.

Ryan dropped his head into his hands, groaning. "That poor kid." He looked up, his hazel eyes agonized. "How did she ever escape that?"

It sounded so simple. "One day a guy pulled up to the curb where Devony was working the street, but instead of paying her for sex, he paid her to sit in his car and read a tract that explained how God sees sin and how to be free of it. He prayed with her right there." A day or so later, Devony had managed to get to a police station. She had just turned seventeen. Eventually, her pimp and his phalanx of enforcers had gone to jail. "It took a long time and a lot of counseling," Ivy went on, "but eventually Devony got clean and straight, and that's when she got the idea for the Web site."

"She counsels others in the same situation?" Ryan asked.

"Actually, what she does is get Christian psychologists and other professionals to do it for free. There's lots of other stuff going on there, too, lots of resources available."

"So how did you two meet?" Ryan asked.

Ivy sighed. "When I read her story and saw what she's doing, I suggested to Brand that we do a show with her. I was always trying to schedule more inspirational content, but usually he shot down my ideas. This time, though, he went for it.

Which should have been my first clue." Ivy raised both hands, palm out, to make an important point. "I scripted what I thought was a very uplifting, important show, but when it came air time, Brand savaged her. He only wanted the gory details."

A muscle jerked in the hollow of Ryan's jaw. "Man, what a scuzzball."

Ivy couldn't have agreed more. "It was the worst. He humiliated her. I shut off my mic and left the booth, but through it all Devony calmly used every opportunity to try to witness, to explain her beliefs and give the Web site address." Ivy took a deep breath to keep her tears at bay as she recalled that day. "Afterward, Devony actually comforted *me.* It was like she could see straight into my heart, and listening to her, I knew that I had to have what she had."

Ryan covered his face with his hands. "God forgive me," he moaned. When he looked up, regret glistened in his mottled gold and green eyes. "I didn't have the courage to ask the questions that I should have," he whispered enigmatically. Then he squared his shoulders. "But that stops now." He picked up her free hand from the table with both of his. "Will you have dinner with me again tomorrow night?" he asked.

Delight washed over Ivy, and she nodded happily. "I'll have dinner with you again tomorrow evening," she said, "on one condition."

His smile skewed sideways. "Let's hear it."

"We have to have our dessert first. At Rose's. Tomorrow is Hunter's birthday, and she made a point of saying that he would like to have you at the party."

Ryan sat back, her hand snuggled into his. "Yeah?"

"Will you go?"

"Wouldn't miss it," he told her, squeezing her hand.

Smiling and still holding hands, they discussed the particulars and caught up on each other's lives. Then Ivy stood.

"I'd better call Rose and let her know we'll both be there tomorrow," Ivy said, reaching into her purse for her phone.

"What about your dad?" he asked.

Ivy stilled. "Apparently, he refuses to come if I'm going to."

Glowering, Ryan rumbled, "Someone needs to have a serious talk with that man."

"No, no," she refuted softly. "He's entitled to his feelings, Ryan. I just pray that with time the relationship will heal."

Ryan opened his mouth, but then his gaze shifted away, and his jaw clamped shut. Pleased that he wouldn't argue the point with her, she leaned in and kissed his cheek before hurrying away, happier than she'd been in a long, long while.

With one hand gripping the handle of a bright green gift bag and the other hovering at the small of Ivy's slender back, Ryan walked from the car to the house on Hydrangea Lane. Ivy looked great in skinny black pants, matching flats and a melon-pink sweater set, her dark hair parted on the side and flowing over one shoulder. Delicate earrings made of concentric circles of gold wire set with black beads dangled from her tiny earlobes and called attention to the graceful length of her neck. For the first time Ryan noted how the top of her head came just past his chin. It seemed a perfect height for a woman. In fact, everything about her seemed perfect today.

Ryan suspected that he might be suffering the first throes of infatuation. He had not felt like this, in fact, since he'd developed a secret crush on Mary Alice Whitesall in fourth grade. She and her bright red ringlets had moved away in midterm, and he had been heartbroken right up to baseball season. That had been the year he'd discovered that he could hit a baseball almost as hard as he could hit a linebacker. He hadn't thought of Mary Alice since then, he realized with a slight pang. Something told him that Ivy would not be so easy to forget.

Rose met them at the door with beaming smiles and warm hugs. Despite the shadows that lurked behind her gaze, she looked healthy, strong and pretty in neat jeans and a turquoise blouse, her brown hair piled on top of her head in a froth of waves. She put her head close to her sister's and whispered, "Dad's here, but don't worry. It's going to be fine."

Ivy shot Ryan a troubled glance. Instinctively, he stepped closer and slid his arm about her waist. He would not allow Olie to attack her again. It was that simple. Ivy must have understood, because she smiled at him gratefully, and his heart swelled.

Rose went ahead of them into the family room, announcing brightly, "Look who's here!"

The boys were on the floor, as usual, already playing with one of the birthday gifts, a set of toy farm equipment, as Olie watched indulgently from the easy chair. Wrapping paper littered the area around them and scattered as they shot across the room to throw themselves at the newcomers.

"Aunt Ivy! Mr. Jefford!"

Ryan spared a hard glance for Olie, whose expression abruptly shuttered, before sweeping Scott up in one arm, while Ivy bent and engulfed a bouncing Hunter in a big hug. Suddenly realizing that there were more gifts to be had, Hunter jerked away to snatch Ivy's package with one hand and Ryan's bag with the other.

"Hold on," Ryan warned, keeping a hold on the handle of the gift bag. "There's a little something in there for your brother, too."

"Me?" Scott squealed, instantly bucking to get down. Ryan set him on his feet.

Ivy's gift went by the wayside as the boys ripped into the bag while Rose laughed. Daniel, Ryan noticed, turned and went into the kitchen. Olie sat like a stone, frowning, his gaze averted. Sensing Ivy's unease, Ryan stayed close to her, quite literally standing guard, ready to throw himself into the fray should Olie seek to cause another disturbance.

It was bad enough, Ryan reflected, that Olie had gotten away thus far with spreading those vicious, filthy rumors about her, rumors Ryan prayed she would never hear. Why should she have to know? He'd just keep her away from any place where she might hear them until the talk had died down, as surely it must. No reasonable person could believe what was being said about her.

Hunter seemed pleased with his video game and action figure, while Scott crowed over his animated movie on DVD. Ryan said a silent prayer of relief. He hadn't had time to shop outside of Eden, which meant he'd only had the scant offerings at Booker's from which to choose. Both boys dutifully thanked him before Hunter turned to Ivy's gift.

Going down on her haunches, she watched him shred the paper and dig into the box. Shrieking with glee, he produced a miniature toy karaoke system, complete with working microphone.

"Oh, my word, what have you done to us?" Rose joked as Ivy showed Hunter how to turn it on.

Olie humphed, muttering, "That's the least of it."

Ryan trained a scowl on him, but the older man had already turned his head away and lapsed back into silence.

Rose moved to Ivy's side and placed a comforting hand on her shoulder. "Help me get the cake ready?"

Nodding, Ivy rose and followed her sister into the kitchen. Ryan sat down on the couch and listened to an impromptu concert that had more screeching, grunting and blowing raspberries than actual singing. To Ryan's surprise, Olie seemed to enjoy the show, encouraging the boys even as Daniel called sharp warnings from the kitchen to tone down. Apparently, for his grandsons' sakes Olie would tolerate even Ivy and her gifts.

For the first time, Ryan wondered what Olie hoped to gain by spreading such ugly gossip about his own daughter. He dropped the thought as others began to arrive, members of Daniel's family Ryan knew only in passing, if at all. Daniel came out to greet them, walking right past Ryan without saying a word. It occurred to him that Dan hadn't spoken since their arrival, but with chaos building to a crescendo around them, it didn't seem important.

By the time the candles had been blown out, "Happy Birthday" sung, the cake served and eaten and all the presents opened, Ryan's ears were ringing. At least when supervising a school function, he mused, he could impose some level of order. Here he could only endure the clamor of the chaos, not to mention Olie's angry glowers. He sprang up from the sofa the instant Ivy suggested that they go. If her own smile seemed a bit strained, Ryan chalked it up to her father's sullenness and the din of children running through the house screaming at the top of their lungs.

Rose saw them out just as she had seen them in, with hugs and smiles and whispers of thanks. "I'm so glad you came," she said, looking at her sister. "Don't mind Danny today. He gets in these moods. It has nothing to do with you."

Ryan wasn't so sure about that, but he remained determined to spare Ivy the knowledge of the rumors going round if he could. He wondered if even Rose was trying to do the same. His arm tightened around Ivy's shoulders, he knew he would do just about anything to protect this woman. That's how deep his…infatuation…was.

"Well, that went better than it could have," Ivy commented brightly as they drove through town toward Highway 81.

In truth, the party had been some of the most intensely uncomfortable hours of her life. Her father's unexpected presence had definitely put a damper on the party for her. His disdain could not have been more obvious, but at least he hadn't made a scene. A few snide remarks meant nothing compared to what he might have done and said. If not for her long-suffering sister and the great loss that Rose had so recently been through, Ivy felt sure that the afternoon would have gone much more roughly.

Ryan made a noncommittal noise and shot her a smile. He had been the one truly bright spot in the whole day for Ivy, though Rose had tried, God love her, to make a normal family party of it.

Dear Rose. Ivy had never loved her sister more than at that moment. To think that, after all Rose herself had been through, she would stand up for her wayward big sister against their father both humbled and amazed Ivy. Even if their father never forgave her, Rose's unswerving love and loyalty, after all these years of neglect, made coming back to Eden worthwhile.

It was Ryan, though, who truly gave her hope. Their growing closeness meant more to her than he might ever know. Because of his acceptance of her she could finally envision what a new life might eventually look like.

Ivy settled back in her seat with a sigh, releasing the tension that had gripped her.

"Thank you for taking me to dinner, Ryan. After the week I've had, I really needed something to lift my spirits."

The moment the words left her mouth, she wished them back. Ryan's smile turned to a frown.

"What do you mean? What's wrong? Has someone said something to upset you?"

"Only my boss," she muttered, displeased with herself. She had firmly determined well ahead of this visit that she would not mention the difficulties that had cropped up with her job.

Ryan whipped the car to the curb and threw the transmission into park, demanding, "And his problem is what, exactly?"

Ivy shrugged, a little unsettled by Ryan's vehemence. "Nothing too surprising really. He hired the on-air Ivy persona, but the FireBrand taint seems to have followed her."

"That's it?"

"Well, yeah."

Ryan draped an arm over the top of the steering wheel and bowed his head, seeming partly relieved, partly ticked and a little embarrassed. She could only wonder what had brought this on and tried to let him know that this latest obstacle was bound to be par for the course for her.

"I expected it in a way, really. Anyone who ever heard the original show would know that I was the straight man, so to speak. It was my function to be the voice of reason on air, to balance Brand's lunatic behavior, but these kooks who used to listen to the old show keep calling in, and that's got the powers-that-be upset. It doesn't fit their target demographic."

Ryan shook his head. "I don't know what that means."

"This station and its advertisers are going after working women with disposable income," Ivy explained, "but most women don't like the wildly manic and controversial stuff that the old show was built on. That's why the boss doesn't like it when these guys who used to listen to the old show call in to give me a hard time the way Brand did."

"Yeah, I've heard some of that," Ryan said. "What I don't get is why those people call you."

"Because they don't want to let the old show go," Ivy said. "They like it when some brash, cocky man tells an intelligent, reasonable-sounding woman that she's an idiot. They just don't realize that it was all an act."

"Was it?" Ryan asked, turning his head to look at her. "Was it really all an act?"

She couldn't lie to that kind, handsome, concerned face, not that she wanted to or had intended to do so. Besides, what was the point, now that she'd stopped lying to herself?

"No," she said. "It ratcheted up on-air, but more and more over the years Brand treated me with the same contempt and derision that were staples of the show."

"I'm so sorry, Ivy."

"Not your fault. Look, I paved this road I'm on,

laid the bricks with my own dainty hands. Now I have to follow it to the end."

"I'm still sorry."

She smiled. "Still not your fault."

He smiled back. "It will end," he told her, "and the road ahead will be smoother."

"If I didn't believe that, Ryan, I wouldn't be here with you now."

"I'm glad," he said, sitting back in his seat and engaging the car's transmission. "I'm also hungry."

"You just ate cake!" she teased.

"I didn't eat *the* cake," he countered, guiding the car back out into the street. "I just ate a piece of it, a fairly tiny piece of it."

Ivy chortled. "I think Rose is dieting, and she underestimated how many her cake would feed, but like I told her, it's all good, because we're off to eat catfish now, right?"

"Wrong," he said, cutting her glance from the corner of his eye. "We are off to a surprise."

Ivy's jaw dropped. "What kind of surprise?"

"You'll see when we get there," he told her.

"Well, well," Ivy mused, "and here I was all psyched to hit the old Watermelon Patch again. I hear it's still jumping."

Ryan shifted in his seat, suddenly seeming uncomfortable. "It's as popular as ever."

"Whole town still goes out there?"

"Pretty much."

"Have they replaced that glass sliding door with something that doesn't threaten to fall out every time it's opened?" she asked, just making conversation while she tried to figure out where he was taking her. He turned the car north on 81 and accelerated, shaking his head.

"Nope. I don't think that thing's ever been bolted in. Then again, the whole building is falling down."

"Good grief, Ryan, that place was falling down ten years ago. I thought surely it would be toast by now."

"The place we're going," he told her, sounding almost apologetic, "is much nicer."

Ivy just smiled. If he didn't know by now that she'd rather eat frozen pizza with him than filet mignons with anyone else, well, that would just have to be her secret.

Filet mignon, as it turned out, would not be on the menu, but Duncan did boast a pretty good Mexican restaurant, and when the hostess showed them to their table, Ivy found her surprise waiting for her.

"Devony!"

The tall thin blonde got up and came to meet her, a smile decorating her face. Although she was not exactly beautiful, her wide grin transformed her appearance. Her smile could light up whole buildings.

Matt then rose to greet Ryan with a handshake and a grin. "Man, I'm so glad you called."

"I'm glad the two of you were free to join us," Ryan said. "How'd the job interview go?"

"Aced it!" Devony crowed.

Matt rocked back on his heels, obviously pleased with himself. "As of June first, I'll be the new assistant director and head of foreign language instruction at The Moriah Academy for Boys. Sounds a lot loftier than it is, but thanks again for the recommendation."

"Again," Ryan said, "I apologize."

Ivy had to wonder what that was about, but Matt didn't seem disturbed. "No, no, it all worked out just as it should."

"God always takes care of us," Devony said, sliding her arm through Matt's. She twinkled another smile at Ivy. "Guess what? We're moving to Tulsa. Isn't that wild? I never even gave Tulsa a thought until you contacted me."

"And if you hadn't contacted her," Matt put in, "I'd never have met her."

Ivy looked at Ryan and explained, "Matt just happened to be in Tulsa at the same time as Devony."

"You remember," Matt said to Ryan, "that state workshop for administrators? You were there, too."

Ryan seemed stunned. "That's right, I was."

"You and the other people from our area went out to dinner, but I ate in the hotel grill that night," Matt reminded him.

"And that's where he heard Devony on the radio,"

Ivy jumped in. "They had the program on in the bar area."

"I just happened to be sitting close enough to hear it," Matt said, "and I don't mind telling you, I was some ticked off. That Phillips is a jerk! But Devony, oh, wow. I was so impressed with her."

Devony picked up the story from there. "He went to my Web site that night and e-mailed me a very nice message, which I just happened to be reading in my hotel room."

"The very same hotel where we were staying, as it turned out," Matt explained.

"The next day," Devony went on, "as I was checking out, I was talking to Ivy on my cell phone, telling her what a nice, supportive message I'd received as a result of the show, and guess who was standing next to me." She traded an affectionate smile with her husband, and Ivy couldn't help grinning, especially when Devony said, "That show was the best thing that could've happened to me."

"And me," Matt added.

"I never thought I'd say this, but that show with you made everything about FireBrand and Ivy worth it," Ivy agreed.

Ryan slid an arm about her shoulders. "That show," he said in an oddly thick voice, "may actually have been the best thing that's happened to a lot of people."

He hadn't specifically included himself in that

statement but Ivy could read something smoldering in his eyes, something that lifted her spirits and made her heart soar.

She brightened her smile and injected a note of irony into her tone, quipping, "Wouldn't Brand just choke to hear that?"

Chapter Twelve

"So the photos were posted as retaliation for Devony going public with her experience," Ryan said, pushing back his plate. He was glad he'd finished his enchiladas because distaste for this despicable act surely would have killed his appetite. He was glad, too, that Ivy and Devony had taken themselves off to the ladies room so he and Matt could have a moment alone.

"She was a kid and so obviously stoned out of her mind that she didn't know what was happening," Matt said. "The good news is that if they ever catch the person who posted them, that character will face a charge of child pornography. What really irks me," he went on, "is that some good citizen of Hilltown had to have visited a porn site to find those photos and send them to the school board, but was that person censured? No, my wife was, and when I think of what she has overcome to be the kind, forgiving, sweet, caring Christian that she is, well, it just—"

"Makes your blood boil," Ryan finished for him.

"You're telling me! Man, I am working so hard on my anger these days."

"I don't know," Ryan ventured softly, "maybe we're supposed to be angry for them. I mean, someone has to stand up for them."

"Them?" Matt parroted, an expression of empathy on his kind, freckled face.

Ryan felt his own face heat, then shook it off. He refused to be embarrassed by his feelings for Ivy any longer. She deserved his regard, just as Devony did.

Oh, why was he kidding himself? His feelings for Ivy did not compare even remotely to his respect of Devony. He worried about Ivy as he had never worried about anyone else.

Leaning a little closer to Matt, he muttered, "You won't believe the rumors that are going around about Ivy. They're vile, truly vile, and the worst of it is, her father seems to be the one spreading the dirt."

Matt sat back with a thump. "And who are the gossips going to believe, her friends or her family? Aw, man." He glanced past Ryan and suddenly slouched, a studied pose of relaxation. "Here they come."

Ryan loosened his shoulders, whispering, "She doesn't know, okay?"

Matt nodded and rose as the women neared the table. Ryan noticed that Matt afforded his wife every courtesy, and it pleased Ryan very much to follow suit. He'd thought that he and Hap and Ryan were the last to cling to this particular show of respect, not that they did it all the time in every situation. Still, to stand when a lady approached remained the act of a gentleman. The women, however, did not take their seats. Instead, Devony looked at her husband.

"Sweetie, we'd better go. I think I need to run over my notes again before I sleep."

"Dev's been invited to speak at one of the local churches tomorrow," Matt announced proudly. "We're hoping they'll pledge support for the counseling ministry."

"I'll be praying for you," Ivy told her, kissing her friend's pale cheek.

"Ditto. Oh, it's so good to see you," Devony gushed, hugging Ivy.

Matt started digging out his wallet, but Ryan stopped him. "No way. Get on out of here. Just see you stay in touch."

"Thanks, man. Will do," Matt agreed, shaking Ryan's hand and clapping his shoulder.

The Barstons took their leave with more hugs for Ivy, while Ryan signaled the waiter. A short while later, they were on the road back to Eden.

"That was a wonderful surprise, Ryan. Thank you so much."

"Entirely my pleasure," he replied, confessing, "and not nearly penance enough for having listened to gossip and misjudged Devony."

Ivy sent him a tired smile. "She understands. And forgives. It's amazing really. It's as if God has given her grace in full measure for all that she's suffered and done and she just extends that out to everyone she comes in contact with."

"I know."

"She's such a role model for me in so many ways."

"For all of us," Ryan said.

Ivy nodded and leaned her head against the window. He could tell that she thought herself more in need of that role model than him, but she was wrong about that. He'd always believed, without quite realizing it, that he had suffered the greatest challenge to faith that anyone ever could when both of his parents had died, but he knew now he'd overrated his own trials. The Bible said that God did not test His children beyond what they could endure, which made Ryan wonder if he could have withstood what Devony or even Ivy had experienced. That was a humbling thought.

They made the remainder of the drive in near silence, each caught up with their own musings. When they pulled into the motel lot, Ryan felt an instant of letdown. He didn't want the evening to end. He knew then that he didn't want Ivy to go back to Oklahoma City. He realized how much he would miss her. He would make sure he could see her again tomorrow, before she left.

He parked the car in front of her room, then sprinted around to get her door for her. Apparently, her thoughts were not so far removed from his because the moment Ivy stood on the ground, she asked if he would walk her to church tomorrow.

"You must be reading my mind."

She ducked her head, fishing her key from the front pocket of that voluminous bag of hers. "I'll take that as a *yes*."

"You can take that as an, *I would be delighted*." He lightly grasped her elbow and walked her the few steps to the room. She put her key into the lock and turned it.

"See you tomorrow, then." Opening the door, she stepped up those four inches or so into the room, then turned. "Good night, Ryan."

"Good night, Ivy."

She started to close the door, but somehow his hand came out and blocked it. "Wait."

She pushed the door wide again, backing up in order to do so. He stepped up into the room, decided that was foolhardy and stepped down again, bringing her with him, his hands on her upper arms.

"Let's try that again," he said, sliding his arms around her and bringing her against him so that her head fell back.

He saw the flare of delight in her eyes just before he kissed her, kissed her this time for all he was worth. He poured everything he had into it, everything he'd been feeling these past weeks: the thrill of seeing her again, the disappointment for what her life had been, the pity and the admiration, the confusion and protectiveness, affection, frustration, admiration, gratitude, fear and, finally, hope.

Kissing Ivy woke something dormant in him, evoked something new and rocked his tidy little world on its wobbly axis. It told him absolutely everything he needed to know, things he hadn't even suspected, and demonstrated quite clearly that his own road was destined to be much rockier than he'd ever dreamed.

For one instant of blind panic, he wished he could go back. Then he found himself staring down into Ivy's wide, stunned eyes, and he knew that going back would never again be an option. Against every instinct he possessed, he made himself release her and walk calmly back to his car.

"Good night, Ivy," he called.

"G-good night."

The quiver in her voice and the rigidity of her stance told him that she had not quite found her equilibrium yet. Clearly, that kiss had knocked her back as hard as it had him. Pleased, he considered the ramifications of what he'd just done.

What the gossips might think no longer truly

mattered, not insofar as he and his career were concerned. For the first time, Ryan had found something that he wanted more than he wanted the job at Eden Memorial High School. In his mind, that kiss was a declaration of the fact that he wanted Ivy to be a part of his life. An important part. Perhaps, when the time was right, even a permanent part. He wanted to know that she would always welcome him with a smile on her lips and the glow of delight in her eyes. He wanted to see her at ease, content, happy, and he no longer feared what that might mean. He understood now that he had been afraid to trust Ivy, or any woman, with his heart, which really meant that he hadn't trusted God to help him overcome his fears. Wasn't that exactly what his mother had done?

He thought of Devony's Web site, Reclaiming Purity, and recalled that old parable of the sheep, how the shepherd had rejoiced more over the return of the one lost lamb than the ninety-nine safe in the barn. Grover had once preached a sermon on that subject, describing how, when a rebellious lamb refused to stay with the flock, the shepherd would break the leg of that lamb and carry it about across his shoulders until the lamb healed, all the while learning to depend totally on its caretaker. Never again would that lamb stray from its master's side.

Ryan had suffered the loss of his parents, and God had carried him until he had learned to depend upon his Savior. Likewise, Ivy had suffered the brokenness of giving up her child and incurring the wrath and contempt of her father, and even now the Good Shepherd carried her across His shoulders. Whatever happened, they were both safe in the care of their Master. That did not mean, of course, that Ryan would be granted the desires of his heart, but he could hope, and he could take a stand in that hope, not just as his own man, but as God's man.

Kneeling beside the bed in her room at Heavenly Arms Motel, Ivy covered her face with her hands and prayed.

Oh, Lord God, don't let my foolish heart lead me astray again.

She wanted to believe that Ryan's feelings for her went beyond pity and his natural inclination to set every situation to rights, but a man in his position would have to be an idiot to get romantically involved with her. Wouldn't he? Just look at what had happened to Matt Barston and Devony, who was twice the Christian Ivy could ever hope to be. Ivy's own father would make Ryan's life miserable if he thought anything more than friendship existed between them.

Suddenly she wished that she had not allowed Ryan to accompany her to her sister's today. Olie had held his tongue at Rose's request this afternoon, but Ivy knew that she could not count on that continuing. She didn't want Ryan to wind up in the line of fire.

With any other man she would have shrugged off their few kisses—especially tonight's as simple, if potent, passes, a prelude to an attempt at seduction, but Ryan didn't fit that mold. A kiss for Ryan meant more than that. Surely, though, it did not mean that he was truly considering a serious relationship with her. Didn't he see how impossible that was? Or had he been fooled by Olie's silence this afternoon? Had he not felt the ice-cold enmity that had chilled Ivy to her marrow?

For his sake, she wondered if she ought not to just leave now and never return. It would be so easy to just disappear again. Unless she missed her guess, she would be moving on soon to another radio market anyway, because it did not appear that the current management would ever be pleased with her show.

Somehow, though, she couldn't make herself leave without a word. Thoughts of Rose and the boys and even her father intruded. She had come here to make amends. Running away felt cowardly and self-indulgent, the way she'd behaved way back before her daughter had been born.

The decision to give up her child to a better situation and better parents had been the crucible in which that old, immature Ivy had been burned away. The one who had been left behind had been even more miserable than before, but she'd no longer looked at the world through a hazy film of selfishness. All that Ivy had been able to see had been ugliness, especially her own, until Devony had showed her a new vision, a better vision, a godly vision. What Devony had shown her was the Ivy she could be if she would only let God have His way in her life.

The new Ivy would not run away. She would face head-on whatever God sent into her path, trusting that He would work it to her good, however painful that process might prove. The least she could do was give Him a chance to work.

With that decided, Ivy slept, rising in the morning in time to finish dressing only moments before Ryan tapped on her door. She opened it to find him standing there with two disposable cups of coffee in hand, his coat pockets bulging suspiciously.

"You are a darling man."

"I seem to recall that you take it black," he said, smiling. "If not, we can raid Granddad's kitchen for cream and sugar, but I warn you, the whole family's in there."

"Black is perfect. Give me one minute."

Quickly, she stuffed her Bible into her handbag and slung the twin straps over her shoulder, careful not to snag the loose weave of the bright orange jacket she wore over a closely fitted tan knit sheath. She stepped down next to Ryan seconds later and eagerly took one of the cups into her hands, inhaling its delicious aroma. He immediately produced a napkin-wrapped, toasted English muffin, split and spread with cream cheese.

"Compliments of my sister-in-law, who has us all eating healthier these days. I have another one in the other pocket, by the way."

Chuckling, Ivy took half of the muffin and began to munch, sipping the fragrant coffee as they strolled. "My thanks to you and your sister-in-law."

"She's determined to get your feet under the family dinner table, you know," Ryan commented just before he bit off a huge hunk of his muffin.

Ivy said nothing. What could she say to that, after all? That she'd love to sit down to dinner with his family? That she didn't dare? That she was waiting to see what God was doing in this situation? Every option seemed too presumptive.

Ryan swallowed his half of the muffin and produced the second. While he demolished that, he kept up a running commentary on the weather. The clear, fine days were pleasant and good for the construction of Charlotte and Ty's massive house, he decided, but they were due for rain. Otherwise, the crops and grazing would suffer.

"We haven't had any precipitation to speak of since the ice storm," he mused, "and that was over two months ago."

Ivy finished her half of the first muffin and

accepted another from the second as they walked up Mesquite Street toward the church, but midway through that last bite, she'd had her fill of both the muffin and the small talk. She wanted this kiss business resolved, so she could stop obsessing about it.

"Want the rest of this?" she asked, offering the nibbled muffin half.

His big hand swooped down. "Sure."

"Want to tell me why you kissed me so thoroughly last night?"

Ryan stopped dead in his tracks, the muffin clamped between his teeth, one eyebrow cocked. He chewed briefly, giving her time to turn to face him, and gulped before saying, "Because I wanted to."

"Oh?" She sounded skeptical because she was. Ryan did not strike her as the kind of man who simply followed his desires without careful consideration.

"Mmm." He ate the rest of the muffin, watching her the whole time, while she fought back a number of rioting emotions.

"And do you always do what you want to?" she challenged, lifting her chin.

He lowered his eyelids until only slits of mottled green and gold remained. "If I did, I'd kiss you again right now."

Joy and expectation exploded inside her, followed quickly by sheer terror, because this could not possibly work out. Could it?

Ryan tossed away his coffee, saying he'd pick up the cup on their way back home, and took her by the elbow, his big, warm hand turning her toward the church. "Now let me ask you something. Why did you let me kiss you?"

She first tried to find a way to ignore the question, then studied several possible answers that might let her off the hook. Finally, however, she reluctantly gave him the truth, "Because I couldn't help myself."

"Good," he said, just that and nothing else, which proved to be a wise thing because she couldn't have concentrated on an actual conversation just then to save her life. It was as if she existed within a whirling maelstrom of hope and fear.

She barely heard the greetings of those who had arrived ahead of them, dimly registered the arrival of his family, failed to follow the music, only faintly regarded the sermon and could never remember afterward how she'd gotten rid of her coffee cup. Knowing she was in over her head with Ryan, she kept closing her eyes to pray, but instead found herself repeatedly reliving that kiss. She'd managed to hold those memories at bay, until she'd so foolishly broached the subject herself, and now she could no longer relegate them to the category of wishful thinking.

That kiss had happened. It was real, as real as the man at her side. It had curled her toes and fogged her brain and scared the living daylights out of her, and she had no idea what she should be doing about any of it. Her head-on approach had brought only one confusing emotion after another.

The service ended, and Ivy allowed herself to be herded into the crowded aisle along with everyone else, Ryan's strong hand resting in the small of her back. They worked their way to the door in the rear of the stark sanctuary, where the pastor engaged individual members of the congregation. The press of bodies thinned around Grover as those ahead stepped out into the sunlight. Ivy smiled at the rotund preacher, murmured a greeting and slipped by as Ryan stopped to shake hands and exchange words.

Out on the narrow stoop, she put her back to the open door, trying to stay out of the way. On the other side of that door, on the very edge of the stoop, two women were talking, and every word poured straight into Ivy's ears. It was as if she'd just awakened from a stupor.

"I cannot believe she has the guts to show up at church," one voice said.

"The gall, more like," the other muttered.

"I suppose if you don't believe in God, you have no fear of entering His house."

"Now, I haven't heard that she doesn't believe in God."

"How could she and have relations with all those men?"

"Relations, that's a nice way of putting it."

"They say she discusses it all on the radio, the acts themselves. Did you ever think that someone from our little Eden would do such a thing?"

"You must not remember her mama..."

Ivy reeled away, gasping for breath and sick to her stomach. They were talking about her! That's what was being said about *her?* Lies! And no telling who had heard them! What if Ryan had heard? What if Rose—

Suddenly, Ivy remembered the way Daniel and his mother had all but sneered at her at the birthday party the day before. His mother's lip had curled, and twice she'd appeared to deliberately ignore Ivy's greeting. Daniel, too, had seemed distant and cold, but Ivy had chalked that up to his and Rose's continued grief. Rose reached out in her sorrow, but she'd worriedly mentioned to Ivy that Daniel held his inside.

Chilled, Ivy recalled something else, something Devony had said when they'd gone to the ladies' room together.

"We were so glad Ryan called, and when he said he wanted to get you out of Eden, we naturally suggested Duncan because we had to be here anyway."

He wanted to get you out of Eden. The words had seemed unimportant at the time, completely unexceptional, but now Ivy thought about the way he had shifted in his seat when she'd assumed they would be dining at the Watermelon Patch. Clearly he hadn't wanted to be seen with her where the whole town routinely gathered.

No. That wasn't right. He'd gladly escorted her here to church today, after all.

Because he'd believed that gossip would have no hold here.

Which meant that he had avoided the local catfish restaurant for her sake, not his.

The very idea brought tears to her eyes. He'd tried to protect her. But who, she asked herself, would protect Ryan? Didn't he understand that he could not afford to be seen with her, now more than ever?

"Are you all right? You're white as a sheet."

Ivy gaped at him, thinking only that she had to get away from him for his sake. She stumbled, literally, down the shallow steps to the paved walk below and hurried away, crossing the lawn when clusters of people stood in her way. Without thinking, she dashed across the street. Tires screeched, but she ignored them. She ignored everything, everything but the sound of Ryan's voice.

"Ivy! Ivy, wait!"

She closed her eyes against it, but that voice tugged at her, trapped her. The hand that reached out, catching her arm and spinning her around had no more impact than the sound of his spoken words.

"Honey, what's wrong?"

"I think I'm going to be sick," she gasped, realizing only then how near she was to losing her breakfast.

"Stop and catch your breath," he ordered, once more the authority figure. "Get your head down. Swallow as much air as you can."

He enforced his orders with action, literally gripping the back of her head and forcing her to bend at the waist. She did as she was told, just like his students, no doubt, gulping great swallows of air. Surprisingly, her stomach settled, even as she wondered wildly what the town gossips would make of this. Surely a salacious connotation could be assigned to her standing on the sidewalk, doubled over, with Ryan's hands on her.

Straightening abruptly, she shrugged him off and reached for the only defense she could find, anger.

"Why didn't you tell me?"

"Tell you what?"

"What they're saying about me!"

Wincing, he squeezed his eyes closed. "What did you hear?"

"Enough!" Then, for some reason she dared not examine too closely, she whispered, "There have been no *men*, Ryan. Only one. He was a rotten choice, I admit it, but he was the only one."

"I figured that," Ryan said soothingly, reaching out for her.

She sidestepped, determined to put distance between them, and folded her arms protectively.

She suddenly felt so cold, freezing, in fact, as if the temperature had dropped thirty degrees or more.

"I have to go." Turning, she all but sprinted up the sidewalk. Ryan fell into step beside her, his long strides easily keeping up with her frantic pace.

"Sweetheart, I'm sorry you had to hear that."

Sweetheart. The endearment tugged at the strings of her heart. She said nothing, just kept walking, afraid that if she spoke again she would shatter into a million pieces.

"I'm going to put a stop to the talk," he promised.

"No!" she cried, shaking her head. Whatever happened, he had to stay out of it.

"I should've done it already," he went on. "I just didn't know how best to take care of it. But I'm telling you right now, if I have to break your father into pieces, I *will* stop it."

Ivy froze in mid-stride. "My father? Are you telling me that my father has spread these rumors about me?"

"As near as I can tell," Ryan admitted, shame-faced.

Ivy put her hand to her head, muttering, "This makes no sense. I always thought I was his dirty little secret, and that's why he wanted me to stay away. Now…is he using this to drive me away, to keep me away?" If so, it was working, because all that mattered to her now was Ryan, and the only good thing she could do for him was to put as much distance between them as possible, which she would do without further delay.

"Get away from me, Ryan," she snarled, setting off once more.

"You don't mean that."

"You should have told me," she accused, her heart breaking at the unfairness of it. "Just stay away from me."

She left him standing there gaping at her back. She felt his stare with every step, but not once did she turn. She walked straight back to her room, threw her things into the SUV and drove away without so much as a pause. Hap could bill her credit card for the room. For now all that mattered was protecting Ryan.

Nearly an hour later, out of nowhere and without the least warning, she began to sob behind the wheel of her vehicle. She wondered if she would ever be able to stop.

Chapter Thirteen

At first, Ryan could not grasp the fact that she was actually leaving. Even as he stood there on the pavement of the motel lot, one arm raised in entreaty, and watched her little hybrid SUV turn out onto the highway, he thought to himself that surely she would not leave like that, but that was exactly what she'd done. She hadn't even bothered to close the door of her room behind her. When his family came in a few minutes later, they found him fuming. It was Cara who figured it out.

"She's protecting you, you ninny. She doesn't want the gossip about her to touch you."

Stunned, Ryan literally gaped at his sister-in-law. Nothing in Ryan's life had prepared him for the kind of woman who would instinctively seek to shield others.

His mother had been far too emotionally needy

to think of anyone except herself, her children included. His grandmother, God love her, had been of a generation of women almost totally dependent on their husbands. Charlotte was his baby sister, and his sister-in-law, Cara, had come to town in desperate need of a champion, a role that Holt had ably filled.

After several minutes of reflection, Ryan suspected that Cara was right. Ivy was protecting him; it was the only thing that made any sense. How ironic that she should be the only one to concur with his selfish concern for his precious reputation, now that he was beginning to understand what really mattered.

Later, it occurred to him to check her initial registration card for a cell phone number and address. Over the next few days he tried calling, but Ivy did not take his calls, not on her personal phone and not on her radio program. His voice mails went unacknowledged. He tried to e-mail her through the station to no avail, so on Friday immediately after the end of the school day, Ryan made the walk over to the junior high school to find Daniel.

"Has Rose heard from Ivy since the birthday party?"

Daniel shook his head. "No. Why?"

Sighing, Ryan rubbed the back of his neck. "She knows about the gossip, and now she's not taking my calls. I had hoped that she'd contacted Rose, but I didn't want to trouble Rose in case she didn't know about the gossip."

"She doesn't," Daniel confirmed grimly, "and I don't want her to. My wife has suffered enough."

"I completely agree," Ryan assured him. "Can't you do anything to stop this nasty gossip?"

Dan seemed alarmed. "Me?"

"Can't you stop Olie somehow? Make him come clean about these lies he's spreading?"

Daniel slumped, dropping his gaze. "If I could control any member of my wife's family," he said, "I would have done it a long time ago, but I'll do what I can."

"Thank you." Ryan clasped the other man's hand. "And would you ask Rose to ask Ivy to call me? Please."

Daniel nodded, and Ryan went away hoping that this ugly talk would end, and that Ivy would call so he could convince her to come back home. To Eden. To him. Where she belonged.

It became apparent, on that first Sunday in May, that Olie's venom continued to spew. Either that or he simply could not stop what he had started. Gossip, as Hap said, sometimes took on a life of its own, and that seemed evident in this case.

Ryan didn't know whether to weep or rage when an elderly woman he'd known all of his life stopped him on his way into the church building.

"I'm so glad to see you here," she said, reaching up to pat his cheek with her blue-veined hand.

"I'm always here, Ms. Roberts."

"Yes, but last week you had that woman with you," she said, her snowy head tilting as if in confusion. Ryan blinked, taken aback. Clara Roberts rambled on, apparently unaware of the impact of her words. "It worried me, seeing you with her, and you such a fine young man. I didn't know what to make of it. 'He can't know,' I told myself. But I see now that you've heard about her."

"I've heard the lies that are going around," Ryan said, sure his tone must have frosted the old dear as she drew back sharply, one hand going to her narrow chest. "That is, assuming that you're speaking about my good friend Ivy Villard." Clara Roberts stared, owl-eyed behind the thick lenses of her glasses, as stunned as if he'd suddenly started spouting Swahili. Ryan grit his teeth, doing his best to remain cordial. "Now, if you'll excuse me…"

He twisted his way through the crowd to his family's pew, ill with anger and worry and regret. He asked to speak with Grover after the service.

The pastor had, of course, heard the talk and tried to combat it.

"What was Olie thinking," Ryan demanded softly, "to do this to his own daughter?"

Grover sighed and shook his head helplessly.

"I'm going to speak to Olie, demand he stop this," Ryan said.

"I don't think that's a good idea," Grover told him. "I fear it would just escalate into something you'd regret. Besides, nothing short of a very public repudiation of these lies is going to help."

"It's not fair!" Ryan hissed, knowing that Grover was right but terribly frustrated.

"No, it's not fair, but God never promised us anything of the kind. Just pray, Ryan, and try to be patient until God shows us the solution."

Ryan strove to put that advice into practice over the next week or so, but as Mother's Day drew near, his concern for Ivy grew. Then, on the Friday before Mother's Day, Ivy announced on her radio program that this broadcast would be her last.

"It's been fun," she said cheerfully, "and I want to thank Oklahoma City for a warm welcome, but other opportunities beckon. We've selected a great playlist for the next week, but we won't be taking calls, so this is Ivy telling all her friends, God bless and good-bye."

Ryan bowed his head over his desk and asked God what to do. If he didn't act quickly, Ivy could disappear. Even if she signed on with another station, he might never be able to track her down again. Besides, he couldn't bear the thought of her spending Mother's Day alone. He decided that if she wouldn't come to him, he would just have to go to her, and for the second time in recent memory he left school in the middle of the day.

Ivy sat on the floor amidst piles of paper that evening, her laptop open in front of her. She scrolled down an Internet listing of radio stations, mentally checking off those she wouldn't want to go back to and jotting the call letters and locations of those worth considering on a yellow legal pad balanced atop one folded knee. She'd wracked her brain for new formats to propose, designing shows around catchy titles and quirky premises, backing up her pitches with demographic studies and well-reasoned arguments. Something, she promised herself, would work. No reason to panic.

She had time to find a good fit. Her bank account would hold out for a month or two. Plus the rent on her week-to-week executive-style studio, which amounted to a glorified hotel room, was paid up through the end of the month. Wisely, she had not wanted to sign a lease on a regular apartment, so she'd simply hung some clothes in the skimpy closet here and stashed what furniture she had, along with a dozen or so boxes, in a rented storage unit. She could pick up and go at a moment's notice; she just had to have something to go to, and this time she'd make sure that the radio station knew exactly what they were getting.

Something, she told herself again, more firmly this time, would work out. The few phone calls she'd made had already yielded a couple of possible opportunities, one in Louisiana, another in Tennessee. It made no difference to her where she landed, not now.

"It's all up to You, Lord," she whispered. "Where You lead, I will go."

A Mother's Day card had come in the mail from Chelsea's adopted parents that morning. It remained unopened, tucked into her handbag. She would open it one day, she had decided, when her life had settled into some sort of normalcy, when she did not feel quite so vulnerable and hopeless.

The knocking at her door took her completely by surprise. Convinced that someone had come to the wrong room, she called out, "Who is it?"

Silence followed and then another knock, this time a trio of booms that had her setting aside pad and pen and getting to her bare feet. Suddenly conscious of her ragged shorts and T-shirt, she ran her hands over her head, her fingers fumbling with the loose ponytail sliding toward her nape. Warily, she padded to the door and set her eye to the peephole, but all she saw on the other side was green.

She had never had a visitor here, and she could think of no one who would be calling on her now. It had to be a mistake.

Resigned, she opened the door only as far as the security chain allowed, asking again, "Who is it?"

A man in a grass-green polo shirt and jeans stepped into view against the backdrop of the city lights. She knew who he was even before she saw his face. Ryan!

"Let me in, Ivy."

She put her back to the wall, heart pounding, one hand gripping the doorknob. For half a minute she could neither speak nor move. Torn between jubilation and shock, all she could think was, *Ryan! Here!*

"I mean it, Ivy," he said, using that stern, principal's voice of his. "Open this door and let me in."

She gulped, knowing that she had no choice, but before she could make her limbs obey, Ryan stepped closer, pressing his big body to the gap in the doorframe.

"I am perfectly capable of kicking this door in," he warned. "Don't think I'm not."

She chortled, not because the idea of him kicking down her door was funny, but because the man didn't know how glad she was to see him, that she couldn't have turned him away if she wanted to. Part of her did want to, but another part, a bigger part, simply wouldn't allow it. She couldn't imagine what had brought him here, but it hardly mattered. This was Ryan, her sweet, sweet Ryan. She slipped the chain free, barely dancing back out of the way as he swung the door inward.

He strode in like a man looking for a fight, his hands balled into fists, head down, shoulders squared. His gaze swept the room, taking in the short couch and contrasting armchair in front of the artificial fireplace on his left, the kitchenette and half wall on his right, with the open bedroom and bath beyond. He went back to the laptop and papers piled on the rug beside the chair. Finally, he turned.

"What are you doing here?" she managed, her hand at her throat. Despite the thrill of seeing him again, she knew that this could not be good.

"You wouldn't take my calls."

Torn between excuses and lies, she looked away. It was that or throw herself at him. She found a version of the truth to offer. "There's nothing to say."

"I've got plenty to say."

"I don't."

"So you just run? That's how you deal with your problems now, is it? Just turn tail and run?"

That stung, because she'd done it for him, but he wouldn't know that, and he didn't need to.

"I did what I thought best," she told him, closing the door.

"Best for whom?" he demanded.

She pushed away from the door, suddenly tired, and wandered toward the kitchen for something to drink. "Everyone."

"You don't get to decide what's best for me, Ivy."

That gave her a moment's pause. So he'd figured that out, had he? She continued to the refrigerator and plucked a bottle of water off the bottom shelf, half afraid of what might come next. Leaning a hip against the counter beside the fridge, she faced him.

"What do you want, Ryan?" Her voice betrayed her, and as it softened, so did he.

He stepped closer, his expression open, hopeful. "I want you to come home."

She started shaking her head at the word *home.* "I can't do that."

"I want you to find that courage I so admire and come *home,*" he coaxed.

Averting her gaze, she calmly refused. "I don't have time to visit. I have to find a job."

"You can do that from Eden."

"I can't go back to Eden, not now. Not this weekend, of all weekends!"

He suddenly moved toward her, his arms reaching out. Panicked, she thrust the bottle at him. His steps stuttering, he gave her a look that clearly said he was nobody's fool. Then, calm as anything, he took the bottle of water and tossed it straight into the sink, where it swirled and clattered and finally rolled to a stop. Before she knew what had happened, he had her pinned against the counter, one hand braced on either side of her.

For a long moment, she held her breath, certain

that he would kiss her. Then he straightened and abruptly capitulated.

"All right," he said. "We'll stay here."

"You can't do that!"

"Sure, I can. For now."

Ryan insisted on taking her to dinner. He sat on the sofa in her tiny living area with his back to the bedroom while she banged doors, changed clothes and generally pretended to be irritated that he'd insisted on taking her away from her job search. He smiled, listening to her grumble to herself. After some forty minutes or so she finally emerged from the bathroom dressed in tan capris and a short, sleeveless top made of a crinkly, flower-print knit fabric, the bottom of which rode just below her waist. She wore gold sandals to match the gold flecks in the flower print and had twisted her hair up into a sleek knot.

"You're beautiful," he told her, and she flushed a dark, dusky rose, a smile curving her lips before she ruthlessly pressed them back into a straight line.

Snatching up her huge, puffy handbag, she slung it over one shoulder, sliced him a look meant to make him bleed and headed to the door, but then she stopped, sighed and said, "Thank you."

Chuckling, he escorted her outside. She was trying so hard to keep him at a distance, for his sake, no doubt, but it wouldn't work. The fact that she cared so much about what was best for him meant that they were already connected, whether she wanted to think so or not. He prayed that the moment would come when he could point that out to her and that she would be able to accept it.

As they descended those three twisting flights of open-air stairs, listening to traffic in the distance, Ryan thought of his quiet, roomy house in Eden and told himself that Ivy deserved better than an impersonal, cramped walk-up. She deserved peace and a sense of true belonging. She deserved a home, and he meant to give that back to her.

The Italian restaurant to which she directed him was busy. They stood on the sidewalk out front with a perpetually fluctuating group of other people, waiting for a little square gizmo to light up and signal that their table was ready. When the lights finally began to flash, he ushered her inside to their table in a quiet alcove in the back of the building. There, they made small talk about her job search and all that entailed.

"Have you thought about Christian radio?" he asked, hoping to contribute something worthwhile to the conversation.

She looked down, smoothing the napkin in her lap. "I don't think Christian radio is interested in the Ivy of *FireBrand Phillips and Ivy* infamy."

"But you're not that Ivy anymore," he pointed out. "Besides, you have a testimony to share, an important one in this day of relaxed societal standards. I mean, look at Devony and how she's used her experience for good."

"But Devony's experiences were forced on her. Mine were not."

"All the more reason, if you ask me," he argued. "Think about it. The vast majority of us are in your boat, Ivy, not Devony's. I'd go so far as to say that all of us share the experience of making poor choices at some time in our lives. Don't you think that someone with the experience to back her up ought to be out there showing the world that it's possible to make the right choices and change your life?"

Ivy bit her lip, and he knew that she was considering what he'd said, which was right where he decided to leave it. He had pressed her as far as he should for one evening. He changed the subject to the progress being made on Charlotte and Ty's house and Hap's plans for the future.

"He's going to do it," Ryan said. "He's going to give up the motel. I can see it coming, and so can everyone else. He's agreed to have the Esquivels come to look over the property weekend after next."

"Esquivels?"

"The couple Charlotte and Ty have found to take over the place. They're proposing a kind of lease/purchase plan. Apparently the Esquivels don't have much in the way of savings to help them buy the place outright."

"Poor Hap," Ivy said, but Ryan shook his head.

"I don't think he sees it that way. It's been a tough decision, but these days he seems to be pondering the next generation. I think he wants to sit back and play great-grandpa for a while before it's too late. He'll be eighty-one in August, for pity's sake. It's time. For all of us."

She nodded. "I see what you mean."

But she didn't. Ryan really did not think she understood that the time for change had come to all of the Jeffords, him included, or that in his case she herself might be the agent for that change.

That, too, he left alone, sensing that her desire to protect him would just make her run again if he even broached the subject of their being together. He had to find a way to prove to her that they could be together, if not in Eden, then wherever God took them He had only come to that conclusion himself on the drive up here.

For the first time, he had found something, someone, more important than Eden or the school or even his family. More important than his fear of trusting a woman with his heart. It was Ivy's now; he just had to get her to accept it. But the only way he knew to get her to do that was to show her that he would stand beside her, come what may.

When the meal came, he prayed over it, holding both of her hands in his, thanking God for the food and the time together and asking for the strength and wisdom to do what they both knew they must. Ivy ate in silence, picking at her food more than ingesting it, obviously preoccupied. Ryan followed suit, but his gaze never strayed far from her troubled face.

Afterward, when he walked her back up those three flights of stairs, Ryan sensed that if he tried to kiss her, she would not only deny him but perhaps panic and run again, to who-knew-where this time. So he merely pulled her into a light embrace, kissed the top of her head, and took himself off to a lonely motel room, returning in the morning with a fast-food breakfast.

"Cara and Tyler would not approve," he joked, placing the bag in the center of the tiny table in Ivy's kitchen.

"Nothing new for me," Ivy grumbled, pushing hair out of her face. "I've made a career out of others' disapproval."

"You could change that, if you would," he said, earning a glare from her.

"I've tried!"

"Try again. You have to come home and make your peace with your past, Ivy," he insisted. "If you don't, you'll never know another moment of contentment."

A short, humorless laugh escaped her. "Contentment? What's that?"

"Contentment, Ivy," he said, "is knowing that you are where you should be, right where you belong."

"That's just it," she told him, her voice straining to shrillness. "I don't know where I belong, but it's certainly not Eden."

"Maybe not," he said, stepping close to reach up with one hand and skim back her hair, "but you won't know unless you do this."

"You know what they're saying about me!" she argued.

"And that's why you have to come back."

"I can't!" she whispered, tears rolling from her eyes.

"You can," he insisted gently, wiping the tears away. "You must. Because going back is the only way to go forward. You have to look them in the eyes, show them their lies and trade it for the truth. We'll do it together. We'll face them down together."

"No. No, please. I-if it was just me, maybe, but what about..." She couldn't let him know that her first thoughts were of him. "Wh-what about Rose and the boys?"

"Exactly my point. Eventually Rose will hear the rumors, Ivy, and she'll be hurt and ashamed, with no way to fight for the truth. You think that you're doing her a favor by running away, but you're not.

If you want to help her, Ivy, come back and help me kill the rumors."

"But how?" she asked.

"I have a plan, but we can discuss that later. Just trust me on this, okay?"

"I do trust you, but killing rumors is like killing snakes with a peashooter!"

Ryan chuckled and smoothed his hands down her arms. "What I have in mind involves a heavier, more accurate weapon than a peashooter."

"Such as?" she demanded.

"The truth. It worked for Devony. That day on the radio," he reminded her, "Devony told her story, and look what good has come of it."

"But this is different," Ivy insisted. "I'm not Devony, and anyone who stands by me will suffer, Ryan. Don't you see? It's not worth it. *I'm* not worth it!"

"You're worth it to me," he said, cupping her face in his big hands.

"No. You have too much to lose!"

"What I lose if I don't stand by you is more important." He leaned down and kissed her softly, then straightened before she could react.

She stared up at him, and he felt her wavering. It was enough for the moment, reason to hope and to silently praise God.

Chapter Fourteen

They spent the day touring the city and the evening on dinner and a movie. Every moment, to Ivy, was tinged with joy and pain. Her growing love—yes, love—for Ryan was a mockery of all that she had once felt for Brand, and she knew she must keep him out of the crossfire of malicious gossip at all costs. Besides, she could not see any way to make a romantic relationship between them work. Clearly, she could never again live in Eden, and Ryan would never be able to live anywhere else.

Still, she had decided she would not deprive herself of his company while she could have it. When they parted that evening with a light embrace, it was with the agreement that he would pick her up for church in the morning. She'd been attending a large, busy church not far away, where she'd blended in without attracting too much notice. When the morning came, however, Ivy's composure fled.

"I can't!" she told him, dressed in her Sunday best. "Not on Mother's Day. I'm sorry. I should be able to do this, but I just can't."

Without a word, he swept her up into his arms and sat down with her on the little couch in her living area, holding her while she wept.

"I should be stronger than this," she said after a long while, speaking as much to herself as to him."

"Shh. Cry if you must, but don't apologize, not for this," he told her. "There's time enough tomorrow to be strong, to fight for the life God intends you to have."

"I don't know what that is."

"I do."

"How can you?"

"I just do, and understand this, Ivy, I won't let you wimp out on me. You hear that?"

She nodded.

"Then promise," he said. "Promise me you'll come back to Eden just once more, Ivy. Promise me. And if it doesn't work out as I hope, then I'll never ask it of you again. All right?"

As she looked into the eyes she loved so dearly, what could she do but agree? "All right," she whispered. "I'll try."

"That's my girl."

But she was not his girl, and she wouldn't let

herself believe that she could be. Moreover, she was not convinced that going back would be the right thing to do for anyone. But she would. In the end she would pack up her peashooter and go back to Eden one more time, because Ryan had asked her to.

Ryan left Oklahoma City on Sunday evening with a promise and a plan, nothing more. Ivy still did not know what he meant to ask of her and insisted that she needed the week to tie up loose ends and follow up on job queries. He granted her that week because he could do nothing else, and laid the rest at God's feet.

The plan seemed not only audacious but fraught with uncertainty, but Ryan could not forget Grover's assertion that only a public repudiation of the lies would quell the gossip, so that's what he needed, a public repudiation. Should Olie refuse to back down, then at least Ivy would see that Ryan would not abandon her. Either way, his future would be tied to hers. Ryan hoped, prayed, that he could convince her that they belonged together.

During the interminable week that followed, he worried if he was doing the right thing and spent hours with his grandfather and pastor, talking, planning and praying. Every day felt like a month; Friday itself felt a year long.

Ryan spent the day fretting, when he wasn't teaching, coaching, overseeing graduation plans or arranging to attend a seminar on Saturday. That had been Principal Spicer's price for letting him walk out early on the previous Friday. In return for Spicer covering his afternoon classes, Ryan had agreed to take Spicer's place in the year-end seminar on Saturday. He hated to do it, but at the time his only thought had been to get to Ivy before she disappeared.

On Friday evening, Hap looked up from the domino table where he sat once again with Teddy Booker, Justus Inman and Grover Waller, and announced, "She's here." Ryan didn't have to ask who he meant. He just got up from Hap's rocker and went to the counter to pick up the room key he had laid there earlier. As he went by, he clapped Grover on the shoulder.

He and the pastor had prayed together, and they'd planned together. They'd had second thoughts together, and they'd come right back to Ryan's original idea. Now if only Ivy would agree. At least she'd shown up when she promised to. That had to be a good sign.

"Thank You, God," he whispered as he went out to meet her. Surely, surely, this meant it would all work out as he hoped.

Watching Ryan walk toward her across the motel lot, Ivy fought to keep her composure. She had come because she'd promised and because there was nothing left for her in Oklahoma City, but she truly could not imagine what he hoped to accomplish with this.

Even if he somehow managed to quell the rumors, she could not stay in Eden. She had to have a job, and Eden had no radio station. Still, she'd done as Ryan had suggested and fired off a résumé and format proposal to a Christian station in Wichita Falls, Texas, some thirty or forty miles southwest of Eden. Now it was up to God.

If she'd needed proof of God's intentions, however, she'd gotten it before she'd left the city. The station in Tennessee had called. They were interested in a format she had proposed and wanted to know if she could call on Monday morning to speak in teleconference with the station manager and the head of advertising? Of course she could and would, but first she had a promise to keep. She pushed away the bleak feeling that overcame her when she thought of moving to Tennessee.

Ryan reached her side, a room key dangling from one hand, a smile of welcome on his dear handsome face. The face she loved. He would probably never know how dear that face had become to her.

"Okay," she said, sounding more aggrieved than she'd intended. "I'm here, not that I think it's going to do any good, mind you."

"Hello to you, too," he quipped, completely disarming her so that when he pulled her into his embrace and kissed her, she had nothing left with which to refuse him.

She wound up hanging on for dear life, her hands fisted in the fabric of his shirt. By the time he lifted his head, she could barely stand, pulled to pieces by hope and despair, the desires of her heart and the conviction of her soul.

"Ryan," she whispered, "what are we doing?"

"I don't know what you're doing," he told her, "but I'm saying hello to someone I'm very, very glad to see."

Someone you'll be saying good-bye to again soon, she thought morosely.

"Look," she said, shaking her head, "I've been thinking about this, and I know you say that I have to face down these rumors, but how am I supposed to do that? Just showing up proves nothing."

Ryan glanced away, then caught her hand in his, saying, "Let's get you settled then we'll talk about it. Just don't take anybody's head off until you've heard us out, okay?"

"Us?" she asked as she was being pulled by Ryan's hand back to the driver's seat of her car.

"I'll open the room," he told her. "You move the car. Then I'll help you carry in your things. After that, we'll walk over to talk to Hap and Grover."

At least she knew who "us" was now, but that didn't make her feel any better about this mysterious plan of his, because when all had been said and done, she knew that she would be moving on. Alone.

"You don't know what you're asking," Ivy said, getting up to pace back and forth in front of the pot-bellied stove in the corner of the motel lobby. "Publicly confronting my father will just result in an ugly scene." She folded her arms across the midriff of her pink-and-white double tank top, then dropped her hands to the waist of her comfortable jeans.

"Sweetheart, do you think I'd ask it of you if there was another way?" Ryan said from his seat on the couch.

"It won't be easy," Hap put in, "but it could make a difference when he sees that there are those willing to stand with you."

"Not with my father," Ivy argued. "I appreciate your support, I really do, but I don't see how this can work. What if he just doesn't show up? What then?"

"You leave that to me," Grover told her. "I'll get him in that church building one way or another."

Ivy faced Ryan beseeching him with her eyes. "Look, I understand what you're trying accomplish here. If Dad publicly recants the lies, it will go a long way toward squashing the rumors, but I don't want to shame him. I've done enough of that."

"What about the way he's shamed you?" Ryan asked, an irrational spurt of anger pushing him up to his feet. "That needs some redress, if you ask me."

"But Ryan, I started this. I'm the one who disappointed him."

"And he's the one who won't let it go!" Ryan insisted. "Besides, this isn't just about him. Getting out the truth, setting the record straight, is the only way to put the past to rest and reclaim your good name."

"I don't have a good name to reclaim."

"Then it's time to change that," Grover said calmly. "As a new creature in Christ, you have a right, an obligation even, to create for yourself a name that honors your Lord. We're just trying to give you an opportunity to do that. But, it's up to you."

"Pray on it," Hap advised. "You can let Grover know tomorrow whether or not you want to go through with it."

Ivy nodded but reluctance poured off her. Ryan felt a very real fear. It was not going to work. She wasn't even going to give them a chance. Bitter disappointment rose inside of him, but he fought it down. Whatever happened, he still believed that they belonged together. If God could overcome his blindness and his fears and set this precious lady in his life, surely He would make a way for them.

"While you're praying," Ryan urged quietly, "think of Devony. That day that she went on your radio program changed not only your life but hers as well."

The horrified expression on Ivy's face told him

that he had made a mistake. Just remembering that day and what Brand had put Devony through was enough to make her want to run screaming in the opposite direction.

"I just don't know if I have Devony's strength and courage," she admitted.

"I'll tell you what you have," Hap said in his gravelly voice. "You have friends to stand with you, more and better friends than you may know."

"That's more than Devony had then," Ryan pointed out.

Ivy smiled, but it did nothing to diminish the concern clouding her eyes. Ryan felt a chill that rattled all the way to the marrow of his bones.

"I'm tired," she said, "and I have a lot of thinking and praying to do, so if you'll all excuse me..."

"I'll walk you to your door," Ryan declared, taking her by the elbow.

They strolled out into a clear, balmy night. The first cicadas of the season chirped in a hopeful chorus as they moved down the ramp and out onto the pavement.

"You don't have to walk me all the way across the lot," she said then. "I know you probably want to make an early night of it, considering all you have to do tomorrow."

Ryan lifted a hand to the back of his neck. "Actually," he decided, "I don't think I'll go to the seminar."

"But you have to go!" Ivy cried. "You said so yourself."

"I don't *have* to do anything," Ryan argued. "Besides, I'd *rather* be with you."

She looked absolutely appalled. "I knew it was a mistake for me to come back here." She exclaimed. "I won't be responsible for you neglecting your job, Ryan, I won't!"

Frustrated and fearful, he threw out his hands. "Fine! I'll attend the seminar if you feel that strongly about it."

"Well, of course, I do. Don't you think I know how important your job is to you?"

He reached for her, saying, "Not as important as—" He broke off when she stepped out of reach, all but leaping away from him.

"I-I'm tired, Ryan," she stammered, folding her arms. "Let's finish this discussion later."

He nodded and watched morosely as she hurried to her room.

The decision did not come easily. Ivy spent the late hours of Friday and the early ones of Saturday praying and thinking, thinking and praying. She begged for signs and questioned everything. When her angry brother-in-law called her motel room on Saturday afternoon after having spoken to Ryan at a regional conference in Chickasha that morning, Ivy figured she had her answer.

"You cannot do this, Ivy! Think of your sister. For once, just think of Rose, will you?"

"I am thinking of her, Daniel. I thought, well, Pastor Waller and Ryan thought, that confronting the rumors, setting everyone straight, would be best."

"You know what would have been best, Ivy?" Daniel demanded. "If you had never come back to town. That's what would have been best!"

She couldn't deny it, not that he gave her a chance. Instead, he broke the connection. It irritated her, but at the same time, she understood his feelings. Rose had been through so much, losing the baby and dealing with their father's anger toward Ivy. She thought she'd heard Rose in the background just before Daniel had hung up on her, but Ivy hoped not. She hadn't wanted to tell her sister that she was in town until she'd decided what to do. Now she wondered if it wouldn't be best to slip away again before Rose realized she'd been there.

Just as she didn't see what purpose defending herself would serve, Ivy could see no purpose in involving her sister in more of her personal drama. A public confrontation would just keep the whole ugly mess alive in everyone's minds and hurt Rose more. Besides, if Olie stuck to his guns, why would anyone believe her?

Olie had won this battle, and he was always going to. All he'd ever had to do was tell her that he didn't want her in his life. It was what she had expected, really. Oh, she had hoped for more, but she'd expected him to refuse her apologies and tell her to go away. Besides, even if her father could forgive her, she would never be more than a visitor in Eden. So why put everyone through a public battle?

Both Ryan and Rose would have to live with the results and the memory of any such confrontation. In that, God had been merciful to her, because she definitely would be leaving here. Even if her father did back down, and she could not believe that he might, her job search would determine where she ultimately wound up.

No, what she really had to decide was what was best for those she loved, including the man she could never have. How many more ways did God have to make His will known? First Tennessee and now this.

Okay, Lord, she prayed, awash with twin waves of relief and grief, *if this is Your will, then so be it.*

She went out to give Hap her decision, because Ryan was not expected until late.

Hap Jefford was a big, rawboned man, even at eighty. Despite stooped shoulders and knotted hands, speckled skin and thinning, faded reddish hair that clearly showed his age, he gave the impression of solidity and strength. Ivy had never seen much of Hap in Ryan, but when she sat at his dining table that day, his big black Bible between them, and looked into his eyes, she saw Ryan there. She saw other things, too, pity and a slight censure, disappointment.

"Daniel's right. I just can't do it," she told him, not quite able to hold that mottled gaze. "It wouldn't be fair to Rose."

Hap clucked his tongue and sighed. "What about Ryan? What about what's fair to him?"

"The less connection Ryan has to me, the better off he will be," she said, averting her gaze.

"I don't think that's how he sees it. I think he's looking at the two of you together."

A part of her rejoiced. Another part laughed in derision. Steeling herself, she shook her head. "That's never going to happen. You know it as well as I do. I can't stay here in Eden, and he can't leave. His life is here. It's all he's ever wanted."

"Things change."

"Some things do," she agreed. "I'm living proof of it. But some things don't. My dad's proof of that."

"So you won't even try," Hap accused, "not even for Ryan's sake."

"Don't you see? It's for Ryan's sake and Rose's and even Dad's that I won't, can't, publicly confront my father in church tomorrow. It would just do more harm than good, and the end result will be the same."

Finally Hap nodded. "I had hoped for more. My grandson had hoped for more. But I guess you've got to do what you think best. I'm sure he'll be around to speak to you when he gets in from his conference."

Ivy wept inside. *God in heaven, can't You spare*

me even that? "I'd rather not see him, if you must know," she said to Hap. "This is hard enough as it is."

Hap pursed his lips. "Loving someone you're determined not to have is always difficult, I imagine."

Leaping to her feet, Ivy glared at him, her chest heaving. "I never said that. I never said it, and I never will. And if you tell him that, I'll deny it!"

"Ivy, Ivy," Hap rasped, shaking his head, "don't you know that love doesn't cease to exist just because you don't say it? Real love just is. Like the love of Christ Jesus, it's always there, waiting to be given and accepted. Love doesn't promise us any happy endings in this life, but it doesn't work to bring us sad ones, either. Love, Ivy, is what we make of it."

Could that be true? she wondered. Yet, even so, she'd made such a hash of love before. Why would God give her a second chance now? She shook her head.

Hap sighed. "I'll tell Ryan and Grover not to count on you."

"Thank you."

"You'll stay on a few days, won't you? Until you know where you're headed next?"

"I-I'm not sure."

"Well, whatever you decide. You're always welcome here, Ivy."

"Thank you, Mr. Jefford."

"Of course, I may not be here too much longer myself," he went on, smiling. "Time to hand over the reins, I expect. Maybe that's what we both need to do, just hand over the reins to God."

Nodding, she hurried away, telling herself sternly, *No more tears. No more!* She would not weep for herself anymore. She'd had enough moaning and regretting and self-flagellation. She'd done what she thought best. No one could ask anymore of her. The rest, she told herself, was strictly up to God.

She got back to the room in time to catch the phone, never thinking that it might be business on a Saturday evening. She'd given the number out in case her cell didn't work, which it rarely did around Eden, but she'd never expected anyone to use it over the weekend. She hoped it was not Daniel again or, worse, Rose. Squaring her shoulders, she snatched up the receiver.

"Hello. This is Ivy."

A strange woman's voice greeted her.

"Forgive me for calling on a Saturday evening, Ms. Villard, but I thought I'd take a chance. This is Kay Jayes of Christian Praise and Talk Radio in Wichita Falls, Texas."

Ivy dropped to the side of the bed, her brow furrowed and her heart thumping. "No apology necessary, Ms. Jayes," Ivy said. "How can I help you?"

"Well, I hoped we might chat for a while, but first would you mind if we pray?"

Ivy felt something release inside her chest. "I'd like that," she replied softly. "I'd like that very much."

* * *

It was the most amazing telephone conversation of Ivy's life. She and Kay prayed and talked. They laughed and talked some more, and somehow Ivy wound up telling her everything, absolutely everything. They prayed again, and they finally talked business. No promises were made, but it seemed right on both ends, and before they were done, Ivy felt like a teenager again, hanging out on her bed and having a gabfest with her best bud. In the end, Kay gave her some advice.

"Maybe you should go. I'm not saying to confront your father. I'm just saying that church isn't a bad place to be on a Sunday morning, and maybe showing up and holding up your head is what you're supposed to do."

"You really think so?"

"You have nothing to be ashamed of now, Ivy. Why act like it?"

Ivy considered that. Kay was right. And if Kay Jayes and Christian radio could give her the benefit of the doubt, then why should she cower in her room alone when she should be worshiping God? She didn't have to sit with Ryan. He need not even be aware of her presence. Because he and his family always occupied a pew near the front, all she had to do was slip in the back, maybe a couple minutes late. Chances were that her father wouldn't be there, so she really didn't have to worry. Because she had refused to publicly confront him, Grover probably hadn't even contacted Olie.

This seemed right to Ivy, so she thanked Kay and promised to get back to her after she'd spoken to the station in Tennessee.

"Meanwhile, kiddo," Kay said, "I'm praying for you."

"I'll be praying, too. And thank you, Kay. Even if we don't wind up working together, you've been a blessing to me today."

"Tonight, you mean," Kay corrected with a laugh.

Ivy glanced at the clock radio on the bedside table. Shocked, Ivy quickly said her good-byes and got off the phone. They had talked for hours. Bedtime had come long ago.

Ivy felt a moment of disappointment when she realized that it was too late for Ryan to stop by. Despite what she'd told Hap, she'd harbored a secret hope that Ryan would insist on seeing her tonight. At the same time, she knew a sense of peace, which seemed odd, indeed, because she was less sure now of what the future might hold than she had been when she'd spoken to Hap earlier.

All she knew for certain as she slid between the sheets of her rented bed that night was that God was at work in her life.

She would not ask for more.

Chapter Fifteen

He almost didn't go. After hearing Ivy's message from his grandfather the night before and despite years of habitual church attendance, Ryan almost stayed in bed and sulked on that beautiful Sunday morning in May.

He had known that it was a mistake to go off to that conference and leave her on her own even for one day, but he'd felt that he had to go after she made such a point of it. He'd tried to call her on the drive home from Chickasha, hoping they might spend an hour or two together that night, but her line had been busy, so he'd driven straight to the motel, only to be told that she had decided not to confront her father and didn't want to see Ryan.

Didn't the woman know how he felt about her? Didn't she understand that he was only trying to help her?

Hap had possessed the audacity to suggest that perhaps Ryan was trying to help himself more than her. What, he had asked, if staying in Eden could not be an option for Ivy? What price was Ryan willing to pay to have her with him? To what lengths was Ryan willing to go for *her* career? Those were questions Ryan had already asked himself, and while he couldn't say that he would be happy to leave Eden, he knew he wouldn't be happy anywhere without Ivy.

The question now seemed to be, what was Ivy willing to do? If she was not even willing to confront the lies that had spread about her, then perhaps she did not care for him as much as he had hoped. Or was she still trying to protect him?

Huddled there beneath the covers of his comfortable bed in his room alight with the bright, honest sunshine of morning, Ryan asked God that question and found the answer in his own heart. He simply put himself in Ivy's position. He knew then that she was willing to give him up because that was what she believed was best for him. That, more than anything else, told him just how much she cared, and not just for him, for Rose, as well, and yes, even Olie. Just like her little girl, she would give them up because that was how much she loved them.

He put aside his anger and hurt and truly examined himself. What he found surprised him. Perhaps Hap was right, and he acted out of selfishness, after all.

He wanted Ivy and Eden, too. Could he let go of one in order to have the other? If he couldn't, then maybe he didn't deserve either.

A passage of Scripture came to him then, Matthew 6:33.

But seek first His kingdom and His righteousness, and all these things will be given to you as well.

Ryan didn't really know how to go about that in this case, but he knew one thing for sure. He couldn't do it lying here in bed. Where, after all, was his faith in this? Somehow that seemed to have gotten lost in his job, along with everything else—old friends like Matt, new ones like Devony, his vision of his own future. He'd fallen into an easy way of doing things, never expecting more than he had, never fighting for more. Never having to go out on a limb, face his fears and learn to trust. Even as his sister and brother had embraced new lives and new loves, he'd trudged on in his rut, as blind as Samson in the temple of the Philistines. Unlike Samson, however, he would not find redemption in destroying his enemies, only in trusting God.

He glanced at the clock on his bedside table. It was too late to meet the family, but that didn't mean it was too late to go to church, although he might find himself standing against the wall, given how crowded the place had grown. The boom in the oil business had brought several new families to town, as well as to outlying communities, many of whom had gravitated to First Church. Nevertheless, Ryan decided, he was going to worship in God's house this morning, and then he was going to find Ivy Villard and set her straight about a few things. She would know, at least, exactly what it was she seemed so keen to give up. His love, for one thing.

He would seek first the kingdom and righteousness of God, and leave the rest to Him, gossips or no gossips.

Throwing back the covers, Ryan got up and started to get dressed.

Heads turned halfway up the aisle when Ivy slipped into an empty space on the end of the third-to-last pew on the right-hand side of the church. Thankfully, the stir did not reach so far as the fourth pew from the front on the left, where the Jefford family normally sat. She kept her chin up and her expression impassive as she listened to a litany of announcements, her gaze trained straight ahead.

There would be no staged confrontation, but she would do as Ryan had asked of her and look her detractors in the eye. It proved more difficult than she had even imagined it would.

She had chosen to wear a modest, fully lined, pale pink linen pantsuit, including slacks, sleeveless shell and hip-length jacket, but now she second-guessed that choice, wondering if she ought to have worn a dress. Even Ivy's hairstyle suddenly seemed all wrong to her, childish even, with the sides caught up in a pearly clip at the back of her head. Still, she told herself that she had been right to come—until the congregation rose to sing a hymn and she spied her father, several rows up, on the same side of the sanctuary as she.

Her heart in her throat, she considered leaving, but just as she closed her eyes to ask God what she should do, she felt a nudge from the aisle and turned her head to find the compassionate gaze of her sister trained on her.

"Oh, no," Ivy said, even as Rose's arms encircled her. The song swelling around them covered her softly spoken protest, but Ivy knew in her heart of hearts that this could only mean that Rose had learned of the rumors and Ryan's misbegotten plan to combat them. The stiff, angry set of Daniel's features confirmed it. Crowding into the pew next to her, Rose kept an arm around Ivy's waist and leaned in until their heads touched.

"You shouldn't have come," Ivy whispered.

"I needed to show this town that I'm proud of my sister," Rose said loud enough for those around them to hear. Several gazes turned their way, and Ivy gulped.

After the hymn, they wedged into a pew so crowded that Rose practically had to sit in Daniel's lap. In the distance, Ivy caught the contemporary strains of youth worship being conducted out in the fellowship hall and the light laughter of children in another part of the building. The little church seemed to be bursting at the seams. No wonder they had established a satellite congregation on Magnolia Avenue to help relieve crowding. That was where Rose and Daniel usually attended, but Ivy could not deny how touched she was by her sister's support here today.

Perhaps, she thought, this was God's way of ensuring that their father did not make a scene. He'd been reluctant to do so in front of Rose so far. Maybe this would even be enough to stop the talk about her. For Rose's sake, Ivy hoped so.

She heard shuffling behind her as other late arrivals came in and were somehow accommodated, but Ivy kept her gaze forward, trying very hard not to look for Ryan. The service progressed with corporate prayer, hymns, special music and the collection of the offering. Finally Grover stepped up to the pulpit.

As he first began to read from the first chapter in *Romans,* beginning with verse twenty-eight, Ivy had no idea what he intended to preach upon. Only when he came to the end of the next verse did she get an inkling.

He wasn't particularly obvious about it at first, working his way through a long list of behaviors of those "given over to a depraved mind," offering examples and tying them to modern life. Unrighteousness, wickedness, greed, malice, envy, murder, strife, deceit, haters of God, insolent, arrogant, boastful, inventors of evil, disobedient to parents, without understanding, untrustworthy, unloving, unmerciful…something for everyone, it seemed. Ivy bowed her head, knowing that she had been guilty of more than one of those transgressions.

"But we are not given over to the depravity of our minds, are we?" Grover asked rhetorically, leaning forward. Amens echoed throughout the room. "We who have Christ in us, we who possess the Holy Spirit, we're never guilty of 'those things which are not proper.' True?" This time, silence followed, as Grover must have known it would.

He rocked back on his heels, tugging the lapels of his jacket. "Hmph. If we are not given over to depravity, then why is there greed among us? Envy? Strife? Deceit? Malice! Boasting! Arrogance!" He leaned forward again and pointed a finger, sweeping it side to side. "Gossip. Slander."

Straightening, he looked out over the crowded pews and let that sink in. "Those last two seem pretty tame compared to the rest of that laundry list, don't they?" he asked, then he braced his elbow on the pulpit and literally shook his finger at them. "But every time you repeat slander you murder someone's reputation. Every time you gossip, you gouge holes in your own soul and that of the person you're repeating those rumors to, not to mention those of the people you're gossiping about.

"Lately," he went on, "this town has been eaten up with gossip. Someone says this and someone else that, until no one really knows the truth anymore, if they ever did. I've heard it myself from some of you sitting out there right now. It's gotten entirely out of hand, this talk, and some of you need to apologize because of it. Christ did not take Himself to the cross so you could malign others and whisper about ugly deeds. Instead, He went to the cross so you, we, can find forgiveness, no matter what we've done. It's God's gift to us, bought and paid for with the death of His Son, ours just for the asking. Sometimes, once we have it, we forget that it belongs to everyone, don't we? Even those we're so keen to gossip about."

People shifted in their seats, and one or two flashed guilty glances at Ivy. Her face burned, but she kept her expression impassive, her hand gripping Rose's. After a few more words of exhortation, Grover invited those who wished to receive counseling or prayer to come forward during the invitation time, then he left the pulpit and stepped down in front of the altar. He did not ask the congregation to rise or to sing. Instead, he asked them to bow their heads, while the pianist played softly.

"Some of you need to get yourselves up here," he said bluntly. "Let's get it right with God, people.

It's time to stop this nonsense and get it right with God again."

Ivy bowed her head together with Rose's, aware of Daniel leaning forward to cover his face with his hands. After a few seconds, she heard movement as folks started down that aisle with sniffs and shuffling of feet. A sense of peace infused her, as if the Holy Spirit settled over that place and wrapped it in a cocoon of forgiveness.

Thank You, Father. Thank You, she prayed. *Thank you for forgiving me, and thank You for bringing me here today. Forgive me for not expecting You to protect me, for not expecting You to take care of me and those I love. I won't run again. Instead, I'll let you lead, and I will follow. Wherever You take me, that's where I want to be.*

She kept her head down, not wanting to discomfit anyone, until finally, after several long minutes, Grover spoke again.

"Thank you, brothers and sisters. We've done some good here today, healed some wounds, I hope. All of you who came forward, I commend you. Now, if there's no one else..." He paused a moment, looking out over the gathering. "Let us pray together and dismiss."

Grover bowed his head and lifted his hands, but before he could speak, a figure shot up.

"Daniel?" Rose said.

Ivy looked up to find her brother-in-law on his

feet. His hands grasping the back of the pew in front of him, he trembled all over, like a man with the flu. He bowed his head, gasping for breath, then he stepped out into the aisle, but instead of going forward, he turned uncertainly to face his wife.

"I did it," he said in a ragged voice. "I spread those lies about Ivy."

Rose squeaked in dismay, her hands cutting the sound off as she clapped them over her mouth. Mentally reeling, Ivy saw her father rise and turn to stare at Daniel. Her first thought was to spare him, them, everyone. She could see the shock on her father's face and felt the same emanating from her sister. Sitting forward slightly, she prepared to rise and say—she honestly had no idea what she would say—something to stop this, to deflect it, but then a pair of warm, heavy hands fell upon her shoulders.

She knew those hands, loved those hands.

Biting her lip, she covered one of those hands with her own.

"Why, Danny?" she heard her sister ask.

"It was all so perfect before she came," he said plaintively, his face contorted and wet with tears. "We were happy, and we were going to have another baby. Then she came back, and it all went wrong."

Rose sprang up. "It wasn't perfect, Danny. The pregnancy was problematic from the beginning. You know that."

"But we were okay. Then she came back and upset everything. You had the baby too early, and your father kept saying…" He brought his hands to his head. "Olie kept saying how she was like your mother, how she ruined everything." He started to sob. "I—I think I needed to punish someone because we lost the baby. I told myself that I was d-doing it for you, that if she went away and stayed away we could be happy again."

"Oh, Daniel," Rose said, stepping out to take her wounded husband in her arms. She turned a look of sorrow and apology on Ivy as he wept as he must have needed to do since the death of his child.

Some people near the back of the church rose and slipped out at that point. Others murmured softly. Some wept themselves. After a moment, Daniel lifted his head and stepped free of his wife to look at Ivy.

"Can you ever forgive me?" he asked.

The hands fell away from her shoulders, but she felt the man behind her rise as she did. As she moved forward into the aisle, he did also, and when she reached out for her ravaged brother-in-law, Ryan's arms were there to enfold them both.

"How can I stand here," she managed to say to Daniel, "forgiven and free of all my past mistakes, and not forgive you? Of course, I forgive you."

"I took my pain out on you!" he exclaimed. "I'm so sorry."

"No one has to tell me what stupid things we can do in pain and guilt, Daniel."

Smiling through her tears, Rose grasped Ivy's hand and squeezed it while still holding onto her husband. Ivy sensed movement, someone coming up the aisle, and assumed it was Grover, until she heard the sound of her father's voice.

"This is my fault," he rasped.

Whirling within the safe confines of Ryan's arms, Ivy stared at Olie and saw a softness that she had not seen in many, many years. Chin quivering, shoulders slumped, he shook his head.

"Dan hasn't done anything I haven't been doing," he admitted. "I took out my pain and anger at your mama on you."

"Daddy."

"She was sick, you know, Ivy. She couldn't help herself, and the whole town knew. They knew every time I took her back. They knew I loved her too much to stand my ground and say no more. And once she was gone for good, I made up my mind I'd never be that weak, pathetic man who loved too much again. Instead I became a weak, pathetic man who loved too little."

"Daddy!"

"When my own daughter came to me, I turned her away," he said in a small voice. "Because she'd disappointed me, because she'd hurt me, I turned her away." He squeezed his eyes shut and bowed his head. "God forgive me," he said. "It's eaten at my soul like cancer, and I'm so sorry, Ivy."

"Oh, Daddy, it's okay," she said, slipping free of Ryan to go to him.

Olie shook his head. "Dan blamed you for the loss of their baby, and that was none of your fault." He lifted an agonized gaze, whispering, "But you lost yours, Ivy, on account of me."

"No. No! That was my choice, my decision. I might not have been brave enough to give her up under other circumstances, but it was the right thing, the best thing, for her."

"What about what's best for you, Ivy?" Olie asked softly, lifting his hand to her arm. "What about what's best for you?"

"You know, Dad," Ivy said, with a tearful glance over her shoulder at Ryan's beloved face, "I think I've finally figured that out."

Olie, too, glanced at Ryan before pulling her roughly into his arms. "I'm so glad. Because I love you, Ivy. I always have."

She wept then from sheer joy, and when she felt Ryan's strong, comforting hands again, she turned once more into his embrace, laughing now. The building was all but empty, she realized, most folks having quietly slipped out.

The Jeffords remained, of course, and Grover and his wife, Rose and Daniel, a few others. A little old woman with stark white hair and tearstained cheeks stood openly staring, her hands clasped to her chest. Mrs. Roberts, perhaps? Clara Roberts, Ivy seemed to recall. She supposed they had made quite a spectacle of themselves, but she didn't care. How could she care about something so silly as that?

"He loves me," she whispered against Ryan's chest, and then he made the joy complete.

"Sweetheart," he said, "in case you haven't figured it out, Olie's not the only one. I love you, too."

And she kissed him with all her heart, right there before God and her family.

Epilogue

Ryan shielded his eyes against the October sun setting over the bleachers and blew the whistle clamped between his teeth to call a halt to practice.

"Hit the showers!"

Helmets and shoulder pads clacking, the football team turned as one and jogged toward the field house. Ryan trotted in the opposite direction. On the three days a week when she did her show, *The Voice of Experience*, Ivy always stopped by the practice field on her way in from Wichita Falls to drag him home a little early. "Someone," she would say, "has to do it." Ryan couldn't have been happier to let her.

Reaching the sideline, he swept her into his arms and kissed her soundly. Behind her from the bleachers came laughter. Pulling back slightly, she glanced in that direction.

"Always have to give them something to talk about, don't we?"

"It's all good, Mrs. Jefford," he told her. "I can hear it now." Leaning close, he whispered in her ear, "Mr. Jefford loves his wife."

Giggling, she shoved at him. She had been a June bride in perhaps the biggest wedding Eden had ever seen, so big they'd had to hold the reception in the high school cafeteria. Olie had insisted that they "do it up in style," and because he was paying, "as a father should," they hadn't argued.

They had married at First Church, where the Jefford family had attended almost forty years, according to Hap. Ivy and Ryan, however, had decided to make their church home at Magnolia Christian, with Olie and Rose and Daniel. It was time, Olie said, that the Villards established themselves as pillars of the church. Ryan was only too happy to aid that cause. Besides, he liked the young pastor, Davis Latimer, and his wife, Becca, Justus Inman's granddaughter with the beautiful voice. Ryan had known her all his life. She taught choral music at the high school, and the two couples were becoming fast friends.

Since the wedding, Ivy had turned that wonderful old house of his into a real home, right down to the nursery. When it came to the next generation of Jeffords, the coach and his wife had somehow made it to the finish line ahead of the others, or would come May, just in time for Mother's Day.

Charlotte and Ty, meanwhile, had finally moved into that monster of a house they'd built not far from here. Hap had moved in with them, and the Esquivels had taken over the motel, where their eight-year-old daughter Olivia liked to sit cross-legged in front of the potbellied stove and watch Hap and his cronies play dominoes on the game table in the lobby, when she wasn't chasing after Ace, that was, and trying to teach him Spanish.

Holt and Cara, too, were expecting a happy event sometime around the end of June, and Holt was racing against the weather, trying to get a third bedroom built onto his ranch house before winter set in. With his drilling business booming, it didn't seem likely, so Ty had sent for a construction team all the way from Dallas, the very ones who had built his and Charlotte's house. Holt complained that he didn't want the Taj Mahal, just a nursery, but when the crew arrived, Holt would no doubt put them to work.

Rose and Dan were hoping to try for another child again, too, before long. The doctors said the chances were excellent that Hunter and Scott would soon have that baby sister, after all.

"Or at least," Hunter said, "a stinky baby brother."

Their courage amazed Ryan, and he and Ivy and all the rest of the family, both families, wished them well.

If the past year had been one of weddings, the next year promised to be one of babies, which was just as it should be. Much was just as it should be.

On that steamy August day when Ivy had confirmed her pregnancy, she had finally read the card that she'd received from Chelsea's adopted parents for last Mother's Day. Chelsea was well and happy, it said, a joy and gift for which they would forever be grateful, but she had begun to ask about the mommy who had carried her in her belly. She was still too young, they had written, but one day she would want to meet Ivy. They had wanted to know how Ivy felt about that.

Ivy felt grateful and anxious and right about that, and so, on the bedside table, the Jeffords now had a framed photo of a lovely little girl with dark hair and big brown eyes. Ivy no longer wept over it, but she did hold it against her heart every night before she slipped into bed. Ryan expected that she always would, but she would have their child to hold close to her heart, too, and hopefully several more. He thanked God for that.

"I had an unexpected caller today," Ivy said as they walked arm in arm toward her hybrid.

"Oh? Someone interesting."

"You could say that. It was Brand."

Ryan stopped dead in his tracks and swung her around to face him, anger setting his face like stone. "What did he want?"

Brand Phillips had moved to the West Coast and taken up where he and Ivy had left off with their show. Sadly, it was raunchier and more popular than ever. Even the nightly television news programs had taken to mentioning the latest scandalous topic under discussion. Currently, it had to do with Brand's divorce and all the women he'd managed to cheat on his wife with in the short year of their marriage.

"Mostly, I think he wanted to embarrass me," Ivy said, tilting her head to one side.

Ryan felt his temper spike. "And did he?"

"No. I think it rattled him because he couldn't rattle me. Kay says we sounded like any two old business partners who had gone their separate ways, only one seemed quite content with her lot, and the other did not."

"Hmm."

"He offered me my old job back."

Ryan lifted an eyebrow. "And what did you say to that? Something appropriate to Christian radio, I assume."

"Very appropriate." Taking his hand, she smiled and started for the car once more. "I told him I wouldn't trade my life in Eden, Oklahoma, for anything short of Heaven."

Ryan smiled and pulled her close once more. He meant to keep her there for the rest of his life. They would grow old together, right there in Eden, with their children and grandchildren and, God willing, great-grandchildren around them, and it would be the next best thing to Heaven.

Oh, Eden was no better or worse than any other small town, he knew, but it was home, his own personal paradise, fashioned like the Eden of old by the hand of a loving God for His children. They even had a new cell tower out east of town now. Who could ask for anything more?

Certainly not Ryan, for God had gifted him with far more than he'd ever dreamed possible. Not any of the Jeffords, when it came to that, and, no, nor any of the Villards, either. Not anyone whom God has so blessed.

For true Eden is anywhere that faith and love grow.

* * * * *

Dear Reader,

Whole industries have been built around gossip. We gobble up everything that promises fresh scuttlebutt. Many celebrities actually court gossip in order to stay in the public eye, knowing how prone we are to stop, listen and, worse, pass it on.

Yet gossip is one of the most destructive forces in the human arsenal. Gossip and slander destroy not only reputations and opportunities but, more importantly, relationships. It must seem, when compared to some tragedies, that gossip is relatively harmless, but anyone who has ever been subject to character assassination knows the harm that it can do and how many it can affect.

What is the opposite of gossip? Truth, of course. May you always love in truth.

God bless,

Arlene James

QUESTIONS FOR DISCUSSION

1. Ivy is worried about returning home to attend her high school reunion. Have you ever attended a reunion? Were you happy you went? Why or why not? Describe what your experience was like.

2. Ryan has close relationships with his brother, sister and grandfather. How important is family to him? To you? Discuss.

3. Devony told Ivy that even forgiven sin, though the eternal ramifications are removed, still bears consequences in the here and now. Is this correct? Why or why not?

4. Ivy felt guilt over past choices. Is it possible to let guilt distort our understanding of God's will? How?

5. Ryan felt great reluctance to directly address Matt about the gossip concerning his wife. Is this understandable? What would you have done in his place?

6. Olie was hurt and disappointed by the choices made by his wife and daughter. He had a dif-

ficult time finding a balance between tolerance/permissiveness and intolerance/harshness. How can Christians find the appropriate balance between tolerance and intolerance?

7. The Internet has taken media and communication into new realms, allowing ideas to be disseminated around the world with the click of a button. Considering Devony's situation, is this a good thing or a bad thing?

8. As a Christian educator, Ryan occupies a highly visible position within the community. Was he right to be concerned for his own reputation? How could he protect his own reputation and stand up for those who may have made mistakes? Should he have done so?

9. Olie worried about distancing himself from those who seem to flaunt God's standards. What do we as Christians do when those among us seem to be behaving in ways counter to God's law?

10. Ivy stated that joining the church seemed to deepen her father's resentment and condemnation of her mother and that this turned her off religion. Has this ever happened to you? How and why?

11. Late in the book, Hap makes two statements about love. First, he says that love simply "is," that it exists, like the love of Christ, whether we ever acknowledge it or not. Second, he says that love is what we make of it. Can both statements be true? How so?